As the daughter of rock royalty, Kate Jennings is far from a princess. After her mother died of a drug overdose, Kate went to live in her father's mansion. However, her life was nothing like her childish dreams. Unwanted and neglected, she struggles to adapt to her new life. Then one New Year's Eve, betrayal shatters her.

Tired of ghosting through her life, she's finally ready to embrace who she is. And that means letting go of her past.

Doyle Kole is a big, bad dominant who hasn't kept a submissive for more than a night in eight years. The last person he expects to find in a popular BDSM club is Kate.

When the sexy drummer in her father's band decides he's the one to dominate the damaged submissive, Kate discovers exactly what it means to yield. Letting go and trusting is harder than she ever anticipated.

yield

BOOK EDGE 3

JENNA HOWARD

ISBN: 978-1-7751134-2-3

www.jennahoward.com

Edited by: Alyssa Linn Palmer

Yield contains BDSM elements and is intended for readers over the age of 18.

For My Mom even though she will never ever read this.
I love how much you support me even after you bragged to
the entire neighbourhood long before you actually read what
I write and then you were mortified.
Oh, Mom.
I did ask you if you knew what I wrote.
You're the best.
And now you know what I write.

Dear Reader,

Kate's story has some dark moments. I fought her past hard because I worried about it being cliché, about the triggers it would cause and how I would tackle it. Try as I might, I was unable to change her past because it's what made Kate Kate. So please be advised that Kate's past and childhood is littered with land mines involving neglect, drug and alcohol abuse and rape.

Doyle and Kate also play on the naughty side where it's all safe, sane and consensual.

Chapter 1

HE REALLY DID need to find a pretty girl to beat on.

Doyle hadn't planned on coming to the club. Sheer boredom and his own company had sent him out.

Ten months surrounded by people and the last thing he wanted to do was be with more people. Then again, it wasn't like he had put himself into solitary confinement in his condo either. Ten months of groupies and fans and tweets of "OMG Doyle Kole just blew up my panties" had gotten to him. Ten months of keeping in check because social media bursts of "OMFG Doyle Kole is an asshole who just beat me up" wouldn't be wise. Ten months of vanilla fucking. Ten months of Jace-fucking-Jennings and his permanent case of asshole-itis. Jesus, but he hated Jace. Just thinking of the lead singer of Cyanide made Doyle want to kill someone. Finding a willing sub was a lot safer. Because no one would tweet that he had beaten them black and blue here. There were rules.

Edge was busy. Thursdays usually were. Nice to know some things were the same even though he didn't recognize some of the faces. Not all of the lights had been switched to black lights because one needed to see who one was whipping, but they did run around the railing surrounding the play zone so as subs walked by, whatever had been written on their skin became visible. Edge always made him think of the coliseums gladiators had fought in. In the center of the ring was the play area containing evil toys and devious pieces of furniture to torture willing subs. The second level, where Doyle and others were sitting, surrounded the pit where the aforementioned subs received aftercare or anyone could visit or negotiate a scene on the the couches. A few feet above them, circling the upper floor was the hands-free zone where the bar was, because once you had alcohol in you, you weren't allowed to play but you could watch. Like the emperors of old. He half-expected to see someone give a thumbs up or thumbs down at what they watched.

White wristbands of those who were available glowed under the black lights. Brilliant idea. The club looked like there were pale purple fireflies flitting about everywhere because Thursday nights were for those like him. Single, unattached and on the prowl to beat on someone. Or be beaten.

His gaze landed on a couple. Well, the sub, really. She was something to see as she lay on one of the low, sturdy coffee tables. With her feet braced on the table, a spreader bar was clamped to her ankles and her wrists tied to the metal legs.

Her dom was between her spread legs, his concentration on her complete as he covered her bare skin with artwork that glowed beneath the black lights. Buried in her pussy was a handheld light that made the artwork glow while also tinting the fluids that trickled from her to the table.

Doyle wandered over and sat on the couch next to them, looking at the intricate swirls and images on her legs. Diabolical nipple clamps held her quivering breasts prisoner. Two thin bars that stretched from breast to breast pinched her nipples to sexy dark pink. A blindfold covered her eyes while her hands were tied down above her head. A round ball kept her mouth open and her cries muffled. She writhed every time Jensen Evers drew one of the pens over her skin. Doyle had been handed a pen that would light up under the dim purple lights.

Evers' attention was firmly on his canvas as he decorated the swollen flesh of the sub's bare pussy. The girl writhed and Doyle leaned forward to hold her hips still.

"Thanks." Evers didn't even look up as the girl's muscles tightened, spasmed and the scent of her orgasm filled the air. He dabbed at her cunt with a towel before continuing his work. The man was as diabolical as his nipple bars. "You're in my light, asshole."

Doyle leaned back, admiring the torture. After a few minutes, he reached over to remove the ball gag. Sometimes Jensen forgot his canvas was real and God knows how long she'd been lying there. "Gently, girl."

"Thank you Sir," she whispered.

He called over a waitress and asked for a glass of water, and settled back to admire the naked girl. This wasn't Jensen's usual girl. "No Daisy?"

"No."

The short answer dragged his attention to his friend. Shit. "You two done?"

The marker halted and Jensen looked up, before returning his attention to his canvas. Doyle took that as a yes. When the waitress arrived, Doyle let the sub have a few sips of water. He should find someone for himself. That had been the point of coming to the club after all. "Remember to feed your pretty pet." Uncoiling from the couch, Doyle went looking for his own plaything. He had ten months of pent-up energy to exhaust.

He knew just where to start.

With her arms folded on the railing, Kate rested her cheek on her stacked hands, watching the glowing scenes before her. Some gave her the heebie-jeebies, but some made her heart beat a little faster while a breathless sort of anticipation moved through her. She wanted.

No, she thought, as a dom stood not two feet from her with his attention on his sub, she yearned. A yearning that reminded her of being a kid and being constantly disappointed. She'd think that by now she'd stop wishing and dreaming. *Wanting.* Always wanting.

Sometimes it was the pain, watching it being shared and transformed into something breathtaking. Sometimes it was simply seeing a sub on her knees beside her dom. Sometimes it was the mind-fuck. Always wanting.

The kink. The sex. The connection. God, the connection. She yearned for that the most. Sometimes she felt transparent, even here, like no one saw her. Just a ghost drifting through her life. Twenty-four and all used up. A husk, a shell. Alone, alone, alone.

Time to go.

Before she had a complete emotional breakdown in the club.

She went to ease her leg out from the railing she was perched on, twisting to untangle herself from her spot.

A hand gripped the railing beside her, a forearm barring her escape. She stared at the demon inked in the webbing between thumb and forefinger, a black ring wrapped around the thumb, filling the space between the lower knuckles.

A knee pressed against her back, nudging her until she was back in her original position and the pressure of a thigh pinned her to the railing. She rolled one of the knots of leather on her bracelet, worrying it out of habit.

A larger, stronger hand covered hers, stopping the fidgeting. Still, she flicked her nail against a thin strand, plucking it like it was a guitar string. A thumb flattened over hers, halting even that. The railing dug into her breasts, the eerie purplish glow surrounding her. She took a shaky breath and shut her eyes.

With every exhale, she felt it all sliding away. All the insecurities, that ache in her chest. They eased away into the shadows, biding their time until she was vulnerable again.

Fingers fisted in her hair and tilted her head back so she had to look up and up and up. Dark eyes stared down at her and he gave a sharp tug on her hair, the back of her head resting against the dark, chunky belt buckle. Fingers tapped on her left wrist and she felt a blush heat her cheeks as he flipped the glowing white side around until it was black. All she felt was *yes* and *please* and *Sir.*

Always.

Wanting.

Kate blinked and let the fantasy turn to dust before she focused on the tattoo on his hand. She wasn't feeling strong enough for this. For him. She ducked under his arm and was stopped by his hand on her neck. *Don't,* she silently pleaded. *Don't touch when it means nothing.*

Instead she said the only thing that would bring this to a halt. "Red," she said to her shoulder and she stepped away.

"This world isn't for you, Kate."

She shut her eyes as the words stabbed deep into a heart that had taken a lifetime of blows. "Tell me then, what world is?" She latched onto her bracelet as she made her way to the locker room. The pain in her chest. It was as if he had carved into it, slashing through all her wants and dreams. She sat on the bench and stared at the small locker her purse was in. Leaning forward, she clasped her hands behind her head and stared at her feet. She thought she had more time.

Doyle Kole didn't usually come into the club the day he came home from one of Cyanide's tours, so she had felt safe. No, not safe. She couldn't remember the last time she had felt that, but at least… "I can't keep doing this," she whispered, her eyes closed as she fought down every damn tear. She would not cry. Bend don't break. Bend don't break. Because if she broke, Kate feared she'd never get up again.

With a tired sigh she felt all the way to her decrepit soul, Kate pushed herself up to turn the combination until the lock clicked open. She dropped the lock into her purse and walked out. Time to go home.

Fuck. Doyle thumped his fist against the railing. He braced his hands on the metal and tapped the toe of his boot into the floor. "Fuck." Lifting his head, he caught a glimpse of her as she disappeared up the stairs. She was too fucking fragile for this. Too shattered. Too…Kate.

"Fuck." He pushed off and made his way through the club. He took the stairs two at a time and started to follow her. He stopped and turned into the bar instead. Chasing her seemed like a bad idea. He'd see her tomorrow night anyway. Kate with her sad eyes, her needy eyes, her sad heart and her needy heart.

"Whiskey," he said. When he had his glass, he found a quiet table and stared at the drink. One of his greatest fears was that one day he'd buckle and drink. "Fuck," he muttered as he slumped in the chair and wondered exactly when his night had gone to shit.

"That's twice you've sent the girl running from my club, Kole."

"Actually, it's the third time." The first time had been a year ago, when to his shock he had spotted Kate. He hadn't said a word to her. Her eyes had gone wide and she had fled as he had tried to process that Kate was in Edge. Kate. The second time, just before he had gone on tour, had been a lot like tonight. He had felt a lot like he did now.

Oz Peters sat down without an invite and draped an arm over the back of his chair as he caught the eye of a waitress. He held up one finger and faced Doyle. "She's a wounded one, your girl."

Doyle grunted. "You have no idea." Fucking Jace-fucking-Jennings. He shut his eyes. "She's not my girl."

"Abuse?"

Doyle clasped his hands on his head, unwilling to go into Kate's history with Oz. Apparently his silence was answer enough, though the man had no idea. None.

"It took her about four months to agree to a scene.

It's not something I wish to see again."

Doyle's eyes opened. Oz leaned forward, grabbed his untouched whiskey and downed it. Shit. "What happened?"

"You ever watch ice crack? Hear it pop apart?" Oz stared into the glass, contemplating the ice. "And yet she keeps coming back. Resilient little thing."

Doyle nodded. That she was.

"You're the one who makes her run. Want to tell me why that is?"

Jace-fucking-Jennings. He looked away. "No."

Oz set the glass down. "The rules here are pretty simple, Doyle. Do no harm. Everything's consensual and don't fuck with me. Don't fuck with me. Thanks for the drink."

Doyle sighed and swore again. "God damn it." He dragged his hands down his face and uncoiled from his chair. Instead of going hunting for a sub to break a ten month fast with, he left. He'd already caused one girl to safe word out, no need to make it two.

Kate Jace Jennings.

Damn, he really missed alcohol.

Kate - 2002

"This place is a dump," a man said, the trailer door squeaking open. The floor vibrated beneath a heavy foot that thumped down, as if he was testing it to not fall apart. "Jesus, she lived like this?"

"Who is really surprised?" a second man asked, his voice saying that they weren't really surprised.

"But still...fuck. Stinks like death in here." Something was kicked. "Dude, no one's here. You heard the cop. She's dead. Whatever is going on, it ain't her."

The floor vibrated as someone walked through the trailer. A cupboard door opened and shut, then the fridge.

"Jace, dude, there's nothing here. Can we go now? Pretty sure you can get hepatitis just breathing in here."

The door made another shrieking noise as it opened and more than one person thumped down the plywood stairs. There was a curse and the sound of wood breaking followed by laughter.

Mouth and nose tucked into the bend of her elbow to muffle breathing sounds, Kate stayed in her hiding place. Fast—so fast—her heart was pounding that she was surprised no one heard it vibrating against the floor. She wasn't going to move until silence followed after the sound of a car leaving.

When it had pulled up, Kate had immediately panicked and hid. It was instinct. The floor groaned in complaint as a foot stepped over the stained and splitting linoleum that stretched throughout the trailer. Her breath caught because she thought they had all left. One remained.

Pressing her face into her arm, she tried to ignore the familiar darkness wrapped around her, the moldy smell of the space. She stared at the seam of the wood that hid her from the world. It wasn't the best hiding place because if she was caught here, then there was nowhere to go.

For years she had hid here. The first time had been because Mom had shoved her in here to hide her when she had brought some guy home. Kate had been too small to understand but from this cabinet under the bench she slept on; she had heard all kinds of things, from sex, to someone smacking Mom around, to people drinking, to drugs being used and sold. Even when the cops had come to take Mom away, Kate had hidden here. She slept here now, afraid that someone would come into the trailer at night to steal something.

At her feet she had a shrinking pile of food, hoarded from those who came hunting for valuables. As if they had valuables.

She didn't want to be found.

Kate was so tired of being lost.

There was a thump above her as he sat on the bench. "Jesus, Beli," he muttered. Even she could hear the shock in his voice, as if he was stunned anyone would live like this. He didn't know. No one knew.

Rubbing her fingers over her wrist, Kate played with the dirty frayed ribbon wrapped around it, as his foot scuffed on the floor. Should she tell him she was here? Wasn't that the point? As soon as she heard the name Jace, she knew who was here. Mom talked about him *all* the time. Usually when she was drunk or high or both. About when she had been young and beautiful. Before Kate. Back when everyone had loved Belinda. But Kate had come along and ruined everything.

I'm here, I'm here, I'm here!

As much as she wanted to shout the words, she kept them to herself as she listened to him slide his foot back and forth inches from her nose. She worried one of the ribbon knots back and forth.

He pounded the table hard enough to make Kate jump before he stood. His heavy steps seemed to match the beats of her heart. The door groaned in complaint as it was opened. He was leaving.

She had done nothing.

Holding her breath, Kate pushed on the door and slid out of the hiding place. She wanted to see him. This magical being Mom had talked about when she was lost in memories of when her life had been better.

Before Kate.

Kneeling on the bench he had been sitting on, she edged the faded curtain aside. There were photos of him with Mom. They were also kept in her hiding place because they were of Mom smiling. Kate didn't remember ever seeing her smile. Then again she didn't remember smiling herself. Not a lot of smiles could be found in this trailer that smelled of death.

He walked by the window, his head lowered so she didn't get to see his face. She knew what it looked like though. Mom called him beautiful and sexy. Kate didn't know about sexy, but he was beautiful. Like an angel with his brown hair, though it was a lot shorter now than it had been before Kate. He also had pretty green eyes.

According to Mom, he had the sexiest singing voice that made girls of all ages drop their panties.

She didn't know about that but once she heard him on the radio and she had cried, because he made her wish her life was different: that she didn't live in a crappy trailer, that Mom wasn't a strung-out addict who hated her daughter, and that everything was going to be okay.

Unfortunately she *did* live in a crappy trailer and Mom *had* been a strung-out addict who hated Kate and nothing was *ever* going to be okay.

Kate rubbed her finger on the dingy glass as she watched him walk to a shiny car where the other guys

waited for him. *I'm here, I'm here, I'm here.*
But just like Mom, he didn't look back.
Just like Mom, he didn't want Kate.

Chapter 2

ARMS FOLDED ON the railing, Kate watched a boat make its way through inky black waters, the running lights sparkling in the night. It looked so serene down there while behind her the party raged on. Music throbbed through the windows, people screamed and shouted. Somewhere in the penthouse suite, her roommates were flirting heavily with the band members of Cyanide. She hadn't wanted to come. There was zero desire to see who hooked up with who, but her roommates had nagged and begged and finally turned on the bitch because Kate had the power to get them in the door.

Not that it was much of a power.

As always, Cyanide had closed out their tour in Vancouver. As always, Kate went to the show. Usually she went alone, but not this time. This time her roommates had caught wind of her ritual. They had heard of Cyanide's legendary after party.

The band owned the top floor of the condo building, though no one lived here.

A hand gripped the railing by her elbow. Panic hit her hard and fast until she recognized the tattoo. Fantastic. "I know," she said as she watched the boat sail by, "this isn't my world either."

"No, it's really not."

"I'm going. When you find a world good enough for me, let me know." She straightened but before she could escape, his other hand landed on the railing, fencing her in.

"You've been running from me for a year. It stops now."

Her fingers found one of the knots on her bracelet and she stared at his hands. "I have not."

"Kate."

A shiver moved down her spine at the way he said her name. His voice was low with a hint of threat in it. The promise of a threat. "Well, I haven't. You were gone for most of the year, so it's like three months."

"Kate."

She bit her lips together because the way her name sounded was enough to make her feel breathless. The first time she had met Doyle he had terrified her. Six and half feet of angry, pissed off male. His black hair had been in a wicked mohawk, with a barbell piercing in his eyebrow and a ring in his lip. Tattoos up and down his arms and his black eyes looked at the world with a healthy dose of hate. The mohawk was long gone and the piercings had disappeared along with his drug use and alcohol abuse. The big ball of anger within him still seemed to be there, though he wasn't punching out paparazzi and complete strangers anymore.

To say that he still terrified her was an understatement. It wasn't that she feared he'd hurt her. It was that she *wanted* him to. She wished she could blame the fantasies of those tattooed hands wringing all kinds of pain and pleasure from her on running into him at Edge. But they'd been there for a while.

"Tell me about Edge."

"It's a BDSM club. Just across the harbor." She pointed north. "You can probably—" She gasped in pain when he grabbed her wrist, his grip seeming to press on all the knots at once. Oh holy…

"Breathe through it."

Her inhale was shaky, as was her exhale. Little hot spots lit up around her skin. Five of them to be exact, because even his thumb was pressing down on the knot against the inside of her wrist.

"Deeper. Take it in, Katey."

When her breathing was a little more even his fingers relaxed. A humming was in her head and she was thankful the glass railing was there to keep her falling thirty stories to the ground. Fingertips eased under her bracelet, stroking over her skin, stilling where her pulse throbbed.

"Tell me about Edge and pack away the brat because that's not you."

She tried to pull her hand away, but his grip tightened just enough to make her feel dizzy. It was hard to think as she stared down at her hand as if she had never seen it before. "How do you know? Maybe I am."

He caught her chin and turned her so he could see her face. That dark gaze searched and probed, looking for something. "The day you trust enough to brat out will be a day for the books."

Probably.

"Hey, yo, D!"

She found herself spun around so her front was

against Doyle. He pressed her head against his chest, a hand on the side of her head so she was gazing toward Stanley Park. The stale scent of marijuana and whiskey made her wrinkle her nose as a not-so-sober Anderson Reeve stumbled into Doyle. The drummer barely moved beneath the impact. The bassist, however, staggered into the railing with enough force she was surprised he didn't fall over. She felt it vibrate from Anderson's body.

"Oh hey, look what you found." Fingers brushed up her arm like a spider crawling. Her wrist was released and a grunt came from Anderson. She wished she could see what had happened. There was something oddly protective in the way Doyle kept her tucked between him and the railing, his palm warm against her cheek.

"What do you want, Andy?" Doyle's voice vibrated against her ear. He sounded not so much irritated but unwelcoming, like Anderson was a pile of shit he had just stepped in and he now had to scrape him off his boots. Anderson was the youngest in the band and sometimes she felt older than him and he was forty. For a while he had been sober, but his third marriage fell apart and he had fallen off the wagon. He had a daughter a few years younger than Kate but they weren't friends. She wasn't friends with any of the Cyanide kids. Not even her own sister. Maybe if she hadn't spent eleven years with her mom. When she had first arrived and learned that there were three other kids her age, she had briefly dreamt of friends, but the cold hard reality had been eye-opening. The twins and Anderson's daughter had been as welcoming to her as the imagined shit on Doyle's boot. They had never let her forget she had spent the first half of her life in a trailer and that her mom was a junkie groupie.

"Hey, yeah," Anderson said, his voice slurred from whatever was inside him. "There's this girl who wants to meet you."

"Busy."

"This girl is right up your alley, hey. She comes with her own handcuffs. Do you come with your handcuffs?" Spider fingers crawled up her arm only to disappear. "Hey, man, relax. You need to relax more, D. Hey, hey, you better like it kinky with D, here. Like hard core."

Doyle pressed on her head and somehow navigated her under his arm. "She does."

Her stomach went jittery at those two words as he turned, clearly done with the conversation. His fingers pushed against the small of her back, nudging her away. She peeked over her shoulder as he shifted his weight so Anderson couldn't see her. Well, that was a dismissal. Tucking her hair behind her ear, she slipped inside.

One end of the top floor was locked off and even had a bouncer at the door. The one room open was filled with people and she made her way down the stairs. A hand landed on the small of her back and she flinched away even as she looked up. Surprise flickered through her to see Doyle. He all but propelled her down two halls before he stopped at a door. She watched him dig out a set of keys, unlock the door before she was hustled into a room.

No, she thought. This wasn't a room but a suite. "Holy…" her voice faded away as she saw an enormous bed that was surrounded by two walls of glass. The noise of the party became muted.

"I need to get out of this shit. Don't leave."

He disappeared and she wandered around the bedroom. A laptop was on a desk and pictures of his kids gave the space an intimate touch. His eldest daughter was Natalie's age, but unlike her sister there was a sweetness to her face, not a spoiled, calculated look that no child should sport. She beamed at the camera as she sat on a swing surrounded by fir trees. Another little girl dangled upside down with a joy that made Kate smile.

They looked happy and loved. Willow and Danielle. Twelve and ten. The youngest had Doyle's jet black hair and dark eyes while Willow looked like her red-headed mother. That was about all she knew about his daughters because Doyle and his wife had divorced soon after Danielle had been born. He also kept them separate from the Cyanide world.

Lucky girls.

Black drum sticks had been tossed carelessly onto the desk so she picked one up, rolling it between her palms as she walked over to the sliding doors, ignoring the big bed with its black sheets and mountain of pillows. It was hard to imagine Doyle living here. But there were personal touches all over the place. Movement made her turn. Doyle walked out of a doorway, his hair wet from the shower fell carelessly over his forehead, making him look younger, and worn jeans rode low on his hips while a t-shirt clung to his chest and revealed his tattooed arms. "You live here?"

"I crash here. There's a difference."

She nodded as she looked back out the window. She understood that. Instead of staring at the amazing view, she watched his reflection as he crossed to her, his steps muffled by the thick carpet. "Why am I here?"

"We weren't done."

The man took up a lot of space, overwhelming everything. It wasn't just his size that did that. It was what clung to him. An aura of power and control that she noticed a lot of doms at the club had.

He pushed the door open and she closed her eyes to smell the scent of the breeze that came in. Salt seemed to cling to the air and aside from the party noise, there was nothing else. "Better?"

She nodded as she flicked the drum stick side to side between her fingers, wondering how he knew. Needing some distance from him and his ginormous bed, Kate stepped outside. Now the party could be heard. People on the balcony above them, music coming from open windows. He caught the drum stick and pried it from her fingers.

"You fidget a lot."

She shrugged a shoulder even as her fingers sought out a knot on her bracelet. "Sorry."

"You don't at the club."

Her gaze snapped to him as he leaned against the glass, his hands resting on the railing and his dark eyes on her. "How do you know?"

"Tell me about Edge, Katey."

"*You* tell me about Edge."

He stared at her, then caught her right wrist, turning his attention to her bracelet. It had been one of the first things she had made. Three thin strands of braided leather with five knots evenly spaced. There was no visible connection, the joint was hidden in one of the knots. It was starting to show stress from years of playing with the knots, rolling them back and forth.

Just when she thought he wouldn't respond, he spoke.

"It's a place where I don't have to be this." He rolled his eyes briefly up at the roof of the balcony before he returned to studying the leather. His fingers caressed the inside of her wrist, making her heart thump a little faster while her skin grew warmer. "I don't have to worry about someone tweeting they just had their ass beaten then fucked by Doyle Kole. It's a place to relax with friends. A place to unwind by finding a willing body to beat and fuck. It's a playground, it's a den of iniquity. Tell me about the knots." His thumb pressed on one, hard enough that it hurt. "Take it in, Kate."

Her fingers flexed as the tangle of leather pressed beneath the wrist bone. He pulled her close even as he kept the pressure consistent while his fingers brushed over her skin.

His other hand fisted in her hair and he pulled her head back so she was looking up at him. "Take it fucking in. Breathe it in, hold, let it out then take it in again." She was drowning in the dark stare, in the pain that radiated up her arm and down into her fingers. When he lifted his thumb, she felt her entire body quiver while heat spread down her spine. "Again," he demanded and he made her breathe through it as he pressed onto a different knot.

When he let go, she staggered into him and his hand tightened on her hair so her neck arched, all so she maintained eye contact with him.

"The knots."

"They're comforting." A dark eyebrow rose up as he waited for her to expand. "They're consistent, always there. They…" She looked away, searching for the right word. He tugged hard enough to make her gasp as he made her look back at him. "They ground me. I like feeling them, the shape of the knot and the way it moves when I roll it on my skin, the way it looks. Knots take time to unravel. I like that sense of permanency."

"Why five?"

She studied her wrist. "One isn't enough and six is too many."

High, shrieking laughter drifted down. The noise grated, snagging her attention. He used her hair as a handle so she was looking at him. "Tell me about Edge, Kate."

She frowned up at him. Why was this so important to him? "Why do you keep asking?"

"I'm not asking. If you look away from me one more time, I will bare your ass and beat it, and not in a fun way."

Her breath exploded from her. Her ass tightened in reflex because the look on his face said it would hurt and not in a fun way. She wanted to look away but she didn't. Couldn't. He found a different knot and she gave a soft cry as tingling pain slithered up her arm like lightening. She actually rose up on her toes. Her hand grabbed onto the waistband of his jeans, needing something to hold onto. A hot throb filled her sex as those black eyes watched. "Take. It. In."

Oh, God! It was hard to focus as she grew wet.

"I don't know what it is!"

"Yes, you do. Take it in, girl. Take it in."

She gasped his name.

"There we go. Right there. Take it in. Hold it for me. The next one is going to make you want to come, but I want you to hold back for me."

Her fingers tightened and she felt a trickle of wetness

on her thigh, an aching throb that moved from her wrist to her clit. He let go and pressed on the next knot. She cried out, her knees buckling.

"Hold it and remember what happens if you close your eyes. Tell me about Edge."

"It's the one place I don't feel scared."

"Now. Come."

Her entire body jerked when he let go of her arm and grabbed her ass, holding her up as heat and lightening and tiny darts of released pain raced through her. "Doyle, Sir," she managed before there was nothing but his hard face watching her come. His fingers dug in as he held her on her toes as she shuddered, her orgasm making her vision blur.

His "Fuck" was eloquent and bang on.

Kate – 2002

There was nothing left. Kate stared blankly at the twisted remains of the only home she had ever known. The air smelled of acrid smoke that burned her nose and lungs. Gone. It was all gone. The piddly collection of canned food, her clothes, the pictures. Gone. It was all gone. Others in the trailer park watched the spectacle of the smoldering trailer while the firemen put forth energy to keep the fire from spreading.

Gone.

It was all gone.

Her legs vanished and she dropped down to the ground. She had thought her mom's overdose was scary. This was worse. Far worse. Because she had nowhere to go. She had nothing now. The clothes she wore were the sum of her life.

The trailer wasn't much, but it had been all that was keeping her alive. She hadn't known what she was going to do when she ran out of food, but at least the trailer had been there.

Now it was gone.

Another plume of smoke stretched to the sky and she wondered if that was the remains of her food. Eventually everyone went back to their homes and the fire was finally put out. Not much remained of the aluminum siding. The stairs were gone and Kate could see the melted side of the neighboring trailer through her home. There was nothing.

Absolutely nothing was left.

"Hey kid, you should go home."

She was home. That was the problem.

What did she do now? She didn't know how it burned down. It's not like there was electricity or anything. Probably someone had broken in to do whatever inside. The how didn't really matter, because she was trying to figure out what to do.

They were looking at her. A grubby kid who had lost far too much weight in the past couple of weeks because she was careful with her dwindling food. Some strange kid sitting on the road, staring at the remains of a home. Mom was gone. The trailer was gone. The next thing to go was her. She'd disappear into nothing.

"Hey," the same guy said again. "This is no place for a kid to be right now."

She tried to stand but her legs had disappeared. Her food. Those precious cans of food. She had no money. No clothes. No food. No hiding place. No safe place.

What did she do now? Kate stared down at her legs, half surprised they were still there. She couldn't feel them. She couldn't feel the road beneath her or the cool air on her skin. She was disappearing because there was nothing now.

There was nobody.

Except a name.

Chapter 3

DOYLE REALLY WANTED a drink. He sat on the only private patio in the entire penthouse, staring out the water and trying to figure out exactly when he had lost control. The party was still going strong. He looked at the door when Kate stepped out. Jesus. Could she look any younger? She wore one of his shirts and it dwarfed her.

Delicate, fragile girl. Her brown hair was wet from the bath he had started for her. She was tiny all over, from her height to her breasts to her toes. Those bare toes with their pale pink painted nails rubbed the back of her calf. Great legs.

His elbow braced on the arm of the chair; he studied her over his fist. She looked so much like a young Jace Jennings it was startling. She had the same jade green eyes, but they had a graveness that would never be in the man. The mouth that was famous on her father for his pouts and snarls was sensual on the daughter. When she came, all that hidden sensuality spilled free.

She was twisting and rolling one of the knots as she watched him.

"Stop fidgeting."

She lowered her foot though she continued to absently play with her bracelet, like she wasn't even aware she did it. He crooked a finger at her and she took a step closer, her eyes flicking about nervously. Snapping his fingers to catch her attention, he pointed at his eyes. "Tell me about Edge."

Her shoulders rose and fell. "I did."

Doyle found himself studying her. She blushed and looked away. "We're discussing it again, only without the distractions. Sit down." He watched her fingers roll a knot as she looked around his balcony, debating her options. There was a matching chair facing his and a padded bench against the railing. The bench was always out there, but he had fetched the chairs from inside. He hated having things hampering his view when he was here. Furniture got in the way.

He watched Kate weigh and measure. The bench was furthest away from him so he was curious as to her pick. She tucked her damp hair behind her ear as her gaze bounced from spot to spot. After taking a deep breath, she sat in the chair. She tucked her feet under her ass and adjusted the hem of his shirt over her knees. She frowned and looked around. "Why is it warm out here?"

"This is a twenty-million dollar penthouse, Katey; there's going to be heated balconies." He pointed up where heating panels reflected warmth down on them.

"Cool."

He nodded. "Tell me what intrigues you at the club."

Her gaze that had been on the roof bounced down to his so fast he swore he heard a soft click. "Ah…what?" Her cheeks went pink so he knew she had heard him. "I…what do you mean?"

"What makes the skin at the small of your back prickle? For me it's the Saint Andrew's Cross. A sub splayed out with their back against the cross. They're vulnerable, all those sensitive bits are easy access. The way a sub flinches when a strike from a crop comes close to a delicate area." He watched her face. Her pupils dilated and her lips parted as if she saw it. "If it's a male, I enjoy the way a flogger will dance over his cock, teasing and hurting. A female with her nipples clamped and swollen, her body shuddering if a whisper of air brushes over her sensitive nipples. Arms immobile, legs spread, cunt weeping with need, ass filled with a plug so every time she jerks back her ass hits the wood and the dildo rubs within, making her think of my cock inside her."

Her fingers were still, no fidgeting with her knots now. Against the soft cotton, her nipples were hard while her breasts rose and fell with every shaky breath she took. "The realization that at any moment I can free her ankles and plunge my cock into her while she's still tied to the cross, body covered in red marks, her head lost in the ether of pleasure and pain as she lets me inside her. Deep inside. Not just her cunt, but into her soul. That cross. Fucking beautiful piece of cruelty. Designed to immobilize, to hold a sub open to not just the pain but her pleasure. Are you wet?" Her lashes fluttered and she gave a jerky nod. "Use your words, Katey."

"Yes, Sir."

Fuck. His cock throbbed at those two little words slipping from her. "Beautiful. Now what makes the skin at the small of your back prickle when you sit on the railing and watch? As you tell me, I want your fingers tucked between those pretty thighs. No clit, no penetration, no coming."

He watched her fingers tremble as they disappeared under his shirt. No hesitation. Now that was sexy. He could see it on her face that she was already there, deep in her head where there was only submission. A shiver moved through her and she arched as she encountered her pussy. Her breathing shattered as she sank into the chair, the movement of her fingers fluttering the shirt. Fucking beautiful.

Her lips parted and her toes curled. "Tell me."

"Watching a dom set the scene." Her voice was soft and shaky. "The way he touches her as he puts her into position. The way she reacts. Her body almost relaxing beneath his hands even if he ties her up or is using cuffs. The ritual of how he draws the toys out." Her legs shifted as she caressed herself, her back gently arching.

"No clit."

"Yes, Sir. I know, Sir."

He leaned forward, his elbows on his knees as he watched her sink deeper. Her eyes were closed, her lashes on her cheeks quivering with her touch. Her legs relaxed, parting a little for better access and she bowed, her body stilling, frozen in that moment where pleasure pumped through her body because she found a sweet spot.

"Hold it in."

"Yes, Sir."

Fucking sweetest words. She resumed stroking herself, her entire body undulating now because she was deep in it now.

"Fingers caressing along a crop, hands bending a cane, wrists flicking a cat. Some go right into it, others will touch their sub. A hand along a back, a pinch beneath the ass, a teasing whisper in their ear about how much this was going to hurt. Watching them become one before that first hit, the first spark of pain. Where he's the dom, she's the sub, and both know that they belong." Her words became choppy, her hips jerking, her body straining. "That moment before, Sir."

"Stop. Show me your fingers." Her hand was shaking as she held it up, her fingers glistening with the cream spilling from her. "Now I want to know what makes you go home and fuck yourself until you're screaming into your pillow, your body tense as you come over the fingers deep in your cunt. Fingers back on that quivering pussy and this time you're going to ask me if you can push your fingers into your cunt."

Her entire body was trembling as her fingers slid back into place. Her breathing was loud as she shifted. He caught her under the knees and drew them up so her feet rested on the chair, the glistening folds of her sex hidden behind fingers peeking at him. She arched when he pushed the shirt up, tucking it out of the way. "Move your fingers so I can see how wet you are."

She flexed her hand out of the way. She was waxed bare and there was a tiny little heart tattooed right on the soft flesh above her clit. Jesus. Fuck. Unexpected. He looked away and exhaled softly. "Beautiful," he murmured as he sank back in his chair. His hands tingled, wanting to free his cock, to stroke, to fuck. Instead his hand fisted and he looked at her so deep in subspace she had no nerves, no fear. This was Kate trusting and it took his fucking breath away.

As if she knew that was the signal her hand sank down, her fingers resting against her. "Tell me the moment, Katey."

"Sir, may I?"

"You may but you cannot come."

He watched, mentally taking a picture of the way she looked when she pushed two fingers inside herself. She bowed sharply, her cry drifting into the night as what so desperately needed to be filled finally was. Her free hand reached back to grab onto the back of the chair, her body frozen.

"Hold it in."

"Yes, Sir." Her voice was strained and he watched her thighs tighten as if they had the power to keep her from coming. Watching her battle her body's need because he demanded otherwise was one of the sexiest things he had seen in a long time. He loved the mind-fuck. No mistake about it, this was one giant mind-fuck. He wished she was naked so he could see her all over in this moment. *His* moment.

"No clit, no coming. I want to see those fingers move as you fuck yourself, I want to hear how wet you are by what takes you over the edge."

She nodded. Kate licked her lips, her body straining as she began to fuck herself. Jesus Christ. He wasn't ready for the sight of fingers slowly moving inside her swollen sex, her hips rocking to take the touch deeper, the flush on her cheeks, the rise and fall of her breasts. She was utterly captivating.

"The moment after the last strike, the last cry as she comes. The moment before he takes what is his. The way he looks at her as if he's absorbing every mark he put on her body, the way she goes limp because the pain has stopped, the mind-fuck has stopped. Where the kink fades but the bond is still there. That one heartbeat where maybe he touches a harsh mark or she whispers his name. That moment that is theirs." Her fingers began to work faster. "The moment. The moment where they're stripped bare. That one second as his cock prepares to slide into her. That one heartbeat where it's perfect. Oh. God! Then he….takes her. Because she's his. She's his. Doyle." Her entire body strained and he watched her go over, her fingers buried deep in her cunt as it pulsed and rippled as she came.

He grabbed the legs of her chair and dragged her forward. He leaned over the chair and covered her hand, pushing her fingers deeper so she cried out, her body jerking at the sensation.

"Mine is the moment of surrender. When I know you're mine. Lost in the mind-fuck, lost in the pain. That first moment when you sink into it so nothing matters. Nothing but knowing you are safe beneath my hand no matter what I do. When there's nothing. No past, no barricades. It's just you, pliant. It's just you submissive to me whether it's pain, control or the mind-fuck. That's my moment. When you surrender all to me. Take your fingers out of your cunt."

She was gasping so hard for air, he felt her exhales on his mouth. Her cheeks were flushed, her lashes damp from tears. When her fingers slid free, he pressed his in, making her cry out. She was wet and tight, the inner muscles still rippling and convulsing from her orgasm. He held still, watching her body start to come down. He eased his fingers out of her and brushed his thumb over the little heart. "Now tell me what scares you the most at the club."

He half expected her to say him because she was always running.

"Humiliation," she whispered and a tear slid free. "I can't. I just can't."

Yeah, that made a lot of sense. "Is that what happened at the club?"

She nodded and a couple more tears made a break for it. "I couldn't come so he took me into the bar, made me sit there, as he told others that I was a bad sub and…" She swallowed and shook her head.

Fucker.

Probably a good thing he had been far away.

Doyle picked her up and sat down in his chair, settling her on his lap as he eased the shirt over her. She wrapped an arm around his neck, her face pressed against him as she lost that happy place. "A good dom considers his sub first, last and always. If the scene isn't going right, he has to stop it. If a scene doesn't feel right, Katey, you have the power to stop it if he doesn't. If some douche canoe takes his inadequacies out on you, you give me his name and I will remind him that shit will not be tolerated. You say red and you walk away. We know you can because you did it last night."

A watery giggle brushed over his skin and she tightened her arm.

"If you ever let a fucking douche top you again, things will not end with my fingers in your cunt. You got me, Katey Jay?"

"Yes, Sir."

Fuck. He had known she was a complication the minute he had seen her standing in his club, white band on her wrist.

"But what if you're the douche top?"

"Fucking brat." Her giggles did something to him. Something dangerous.

Shit.

Kate – 2002

Kate tugged on the front of her shirt. It was so new she could almost feel the price tag at the back. Her jeans were new too, as were the strawberry red sneakers. This morning she had brushed and brushed her hair until it was sleek like the faces in the magazines. Despite all the new clothes bought for this moment, she wanted to crawl into someplace dark to hide.

She was going to meet him.

Just the thought left her a little nauseous.

A teacher at school had called in social services shortly after the fire. He had noticed when Kate showed up wearing the same clothes for the third day. That and she had fainted because it had been a long time since something had been in her stomach beside the water from the fountain. She was put with a foster family because she hadn't given names of any family members. She didn't know if Mom had family. Mom never mentioned anyone. The only name she ever heard speak was his name when Mom was drunk or high.

Kate might not have given his name if she hadn't gotten caught stealing her foster mother's magazine with Jace Jennings on the front. Her social worker was called in when it was deduced that all those missing magazines had been taken by her.

She wasn't a thief.

So Kate had finally blurted out the secret she held close to her heart because she didn't want to go to jail, like the foster mother said she would. She had a name to give them.

Apparently he was a very big deal because the social worker, Mrs. Lecia, called some lawyers and next thing Kate knew she was sitting in a fancy doctor's office with them taking her blood and swabbing her mouth with a Q-Tip.

Now she was meeting him.

Now.

Finally.

There was no hiding place for her now. Mrs. Lecia's smile was probably supposed to make Kate feel good. She wanted to throw up.

And hide.

Instead she twisted the knot at her wrist. The ribbon was filthy and frayed now, but she wasn't going to throw it away no matter what anyone said. Once upon a time it had been a bright pink color. Mom had gone to throw it out, but it was pretty so Kate took it, making Mom tie it around her wrist like a pretty, bright bracelet. There was more than one knot now because it kept breaking apart.

The meeting room in the lawyer's office was big and smelled like lemons. The table seemed as big as the trailer had been. One large window gave a view of downtown Vancouver while the other had some of the harbor where a ferry slowly crawled through the water.

The door opened and Kate jumped to her feet. The chair rolled away while she looked for a safe place to go.

"It's okay, Kate," Mrs. Lecia said, but she wasn't sure she believed her.

Nothing had been okay for a long time.

Then there he was. Kate stopped breathing as she saw him for the first time. This wasn't a magazine picture. This was *him*. His brown hair was messy, his face a little pale and his eyes had that red look Mom's got when she drank a lot.

He stopped when he saw her, and he stared at her with his hungover green eyes. She had the same hair, the same eyes, even her nose looked like his. *My dad.* The words whispered through her heart and she wanted to throw herself at him. This was her dad.

Her body froze as he looked at her like Mom did. Kate knew that look and something cracked deep inside. He looked at her like she was this unwelcome thing in his life.

Her dad spoke for the first time. "Well, fuck."

That's when she knew while she had weaved fantasies about a Dad who would look after her, he had woven fantasies that she wasn't his kid, that maybe those DNA tests they had taken were wrong. Only she looked like him. Kate looked just like him.

No wonder Mom always cursed her.

She looked just like him.

Just like Mom, Kate was pretty sure it made him hate her too.

Chapter 4

"FUCK, WHAT A mess." Doyle shut the door, closing away the noise that had chased him in. He handed her a bottled water and tossed a bag of cheezies on the bed. "Someone almost mugged me for those so you better enjoy every one."

"Thanks." She twisted off the plastic lid and took a sip. She was mildly surprised he hadn't sent her home.

"I tossed your clothes in the dryer. I even got to kick some guy who was passed out in the doorway. Bonus." He opened the door and brought in one chair, putting it in the corner.

"How late do these last?"

"Until the drugs and booze run out."

"The cops don't come?"

"They haven't yet. Jace tends to invite some of the residents below us so they can't complain. Five floors down? After that you can't really hear anything except the random person who screams off the balcony." He put the other chair in a small nook and shut the door, dimming the noise.

The bottle froze against her lips as she watched him grab the back of his shirt and drag it off. Holy. Shit.

She blinked as she watched thick muscles twist and bulge as he threw the shirt at the chair. The tattoos ended at the ball of his shoulders so his chest and back were free of ink but for a small one over his heart. It wasn't like she hadn't seen him with his shirt off before. Magazines seemed to love having him on the cover, especially drum, rock and roll, and tattoo ones. Considering how impressive his body was, it wasn't hard to see why.

He even had those sexy diagonal muscles that angled from the hip to the groin, like God was framing perfection. The hard ridges of his stomach bunched as he shoved the jeans down and tossed them aside. Kate's breath left her in an audible puff of air as she saw him wearing those tight boxer briefs that were insanely sexy on the right man and comical on the wrong. Doyle Kole was very much the right man.

Maybe he needed a few covers without his pants.

His lips curled in a smirk as he walked toward her. No, not walk. That wasn't walking. He moved how cats in nature shows stalked their prey. She backed up until cool glass stopped her.

He braced a hand above her head, then took the bottle from her. The man even sipped sexily. "You're looking at me with hungry eyes, Katey Jay." His lips were wet from the water. "I prefer it to those fearful stares before you flee from me." He drew a line from her mouth down her neck and between her breasts. "Let's talk bondage."

Oh, let's. Her knees went watery.

"For or against?"

She cleared her throat. "For."

"Now it's already established you like knots, so is rope a yes?" She nodded. "Use your words, Kate."

"Rope is a yes."

"Put your hands above your head."

Licking her lips, she obeyed, the glass cool against her hot skin.

"Cuffs?"

She remembered her words. "Yes."

"Stay there."

She watched him walk away, setting the bottle on the round nightstand. The drawer whispered open and she almost slid down the window when she saw the glint of silver handcuffs. She pressed her thighs together, nerves and anxiety dancing a tango with need and arousal. The metal was cool against her wrists as he locked both at once. A shaky sigh escaped as her eyes closed. The cuffs clinked beautifully against the glass.

"Mm, yes indeed. Eyes on me, girl."

It took a minute to remember she had to open her eyes. Dark eyes watched her and a ripple moved through her sex at the look.

"Now. Let's talk pain," he said and she almost came on the spot. His lips curled as if he knew the effect he was having on her. He went through the list from floggers to canes to whips to electricity. She was breathless by the time he was done, her pussy slick and swollen.

"Now," he said, his voice low as his chest brushed against her aching breasts, "let's talk about sex."

"Yes," she whispered.

"Vaginal? Anal? Oral?"

Yes and *please* and *Sir.*

"Multiple orifices? How about multiple partners? One cock, two? Will you let me fuck you in the club?" His hand slid under his shirt and she cried out, jerking as his fingers slid over her. "Use your words, Kate."

"Yes," she shouted as he pushed two fingers into her.

"I will *always* wear a condom. If I don't have one, you won't get fucked. I get tested pretty frequently because who knows what toxic pussy there is on the road, hence a condom. Even the day after I get the all clear, I will wear a condom with you. The minute you slip a wet pussy over my naked cock, things will go badly. I don't play games. I don't tolerate them. Do you understand?"

She nodded, grunting softly when he pushed his fingers deep into her. "No games."

"I take this very seriously. Not just protected sex but this. You say no, I will stop. You say something hurts, and I'll stop and make sure it doesn't. You say red, it's hands off. If you're nervous about something, you tell me. If you're curious about something, you tell me. Now I know you're going to have some triggers because of your past." He slid his fingers free. "Eyes on me."

She opened her eyes and he braced both hands on the window, staring at her. "You need to tell me what they are, right now. Because I need to know you can handle this, Kate. I will not be the one to break you because you're keeping shit from me. Now. Triggers."

She wished she could reach her bracelet, find the comforting shape. "Humiliation."

He nodded.

"No needles." They made her think of all the times she saw Mom or Jace jab something in their veins. Made her think of her mother dead. "I don't know how I'd do with knives or blood. Sometimes it intrigues, other times gives me the skeeves."

"Skeeves," he said with a grunt. "Anything else?"

"I don't think so, but I don't know. But you won't break me, Doyle." She was already so shattered apart it was amazing she could function.

"Yes, I will. This is intimate, far more intimate than two people having sex. It's about trust, which I know you have trouble with because of everything. I have eyes and I know who your parents are. It's warranted, so I know you won't blindly trust me. No, ouch, red, stop, I don't know: all will make me stop. Even a flinch in your body will make me stop because you are going to be a cornucopia of triggers, Katey Jay."

"Why are you doing this? Just last night you said this wasn't my world."

"I have been known, on occasion, to be wrong. I'm doing this because watching you surrender to me was sexy as hell. We'll cover more in the morning, but right now I very much want to be inside you."

She gasped as he drew her arms down, hooking them over his head. His hands were hot where they gripped her ass and he lifted her up the glass until they were eye level. Automatically she wrapped her legs around him, both of them shuddering to stillness when his cock pressed against her sex.

"Well aren't you a pleasant handful." He squeezed her ass and rocked into her. She shuddered at the sensation as the shirt was pushed up so the cool glass pressed against her ass, making her gasp. "Are you a virgin?"

She shook her head and found the room spinning as he carried her to the bed. His weight was heavy as he lay on her. He drew her arms free, stretching them over the mattress.

"I like this shirt. I like this shirt on you." He freed

one wrist and drew the shirt off so she was naked. He gazed down at her, then caressed a hand from the base of her neck to her tattoo. She arched at the touch, trying to stay with his hand as if her body craved him. "This is one helluva tattoo, Katey Jay. It's one helluva pussy."

She cried out, bowing as he pushed two fingers into her. The feel of them pressing deep, stroking along her as he eased out, made her jerk. Three times was all it took before the orgasm hit. "Right here," he said as he began to caress the spot that made her entire body snap tight. A third finger slid in and a sharp cry escaped at the stretching fullness. Her hands were pinned down when he braced his hand on the chain of the cuffs, his fingers working her. "Eyes on me."

It took a minute to focus on him.

"Let's get you to that moment we both crave."

Kate arched as his fingers slid within her. It was every fantasy she had about him but better. Ten times better. A hundred times better. Because what had she known? She hadn't known the feel of his hands on her, how dark his eyes were as he watched her, what made him hard, how he made her wet.

"Hold it in," he said, then he pressed down on a hard, leather knot. She screamed, bowing again as the combination of pleasure and pain hit her body. His fingers continued to fuck, pushing through muscles that automatically had tightened. "Hold it in. Take it in. Hold it in."

She shuddered when he let the pressure go, his fingers moving more easily. Knowing what was coming, she made herself breathe deep. A cruel curl quirked his lips and he pressed on two knots. When he let go, it was as if everything washed away as the pain eased.

"There's my girl. Beautiful."

This time when the pressure on the knots came, his fingers kept up their steady rhythm. The pain was there, she felt it, but it was more intense, more a part of her.

"Who knew you were a screamer. I bet you scream when I fill you with my cock as you let anyone paying attention know you are getting fucked just right. Are you ready, girl?"

She remembered her words. "Yes, Sir."

His fingers slowly dragged out of her, making her convulse as he hit the right spot and he eased up on her wrist. She lay there, her body flashing hot and cold as the bed shifted, his heavy weight disappearing. Opening her eyes, Kate watched him shove the shorts down to free his cock. He was a big guy. It was a big erection and her pussy clenched at the sight of the heavy weight, the tip glistening. He opened the drawer, pulled out a condom and sheathed himself. Watching Doyle kneel between her bent legs was one of those dreams she had always believed impossible. Just another dream to turn to dust, but there he was.

His hand stroked up from her tattoo, over her stomach and between her breasts until he cupped her chin in his large hand. Against her swollen folds she felt the firm head of his cock settle into place.

"One more scream." He simultaneously pinched her clit and pressed down on the knots. She screamed, convulsing as he made it last. Made the pain tingle and burn, made the pleasure hurt. Her eyes snapped open as he thrust hard into her, filling her to the point of tiny hurts. "There you are," he murmured and began to move.

She gasped every time he pushed into her. Her legs

wrapped around his hips and he gripped her ass, lifting her to his thrusts. Oh, holy fucking…

"Doyle."

"Hold it in."

She cried out, arching as she fought what was building. The feel of him moving inside her was unlike anything she had ever felt. The press of his chest against hers, the movement of his hips against her thighs, the hot pants of air on her face every time he slid into her. She felt his hand between hers, gripping the chain while his fingers dug deep into her ass as he brought her into those hard thrusts.

"Pain or no pain when you come?"

She shook her head. She wanted to feel all of this. "No pain. No." She gasped, arching as a low sound came from him his hips pumping harder into her. The rhythm of him hammering into her, the almost needy growl and her eyes snapped open as she twisted as something cold and unwelcome hit her.

"Whoa. Fuck."

Immediately he slid out of her and the handcuffs were gone. Her hand fisted as her body jerked and she was yanked off the bed so fast her head was spinning. Cool air hit her face as her stomach twisted and seconds away from a mind blowing orgasm, she was throwing up all over Doyle Kole's penthouse balcony.

Kate – 2002

The bedroom was massive. Kate Jace Jennings stood in the doorway and felt very small and inferior. There was a bed that looked like it was as big as Mom's room had been. How was she going to get into it? Gripping her bag of meager possessions, she gazed at the white walls, the open balcony doors. There was a pretty white dresser that matched the bed frame and a cozy looking armchair.

This wasn't a room for an eleven year old. It was a room one would find in a fancy hotel. While holding her bag against her chest, she began to rub the frayed knot on her wrist, back and forth, back and forth, as she turned to find a huge closet. She had one pink nightgown, one pair of jeans, three T-shirts, a week's worth of pretty underwear that had come in a pack at the store, and that was it.

Her bed would fit in the closet.

The woman, the housekeeper, who had brought her upstairs smoothed her hands over the shiny and soft cover on the bed, fluffed a pillow, then looked at Kate, who clearly didn't belong here. "You also have your own bathroom. Right through here."

Kate followed her into a large bathroom and her stomach started to hurt at the sheer vastness of the room. Her reflection in the mirror said she was not in her world. *This is not my world.*

"You do look like Mr. Jennings," she said and Kate wished she remembered her name. "It will take some getting used to. Let's put your things away and I'll give you a tour of the house."

"Is he here?"

She gave Kate a sad look and that tight feeling in Kate's stomach spread into an ache in her chest. He wasn't here. She tightened her grip on the bag and looked around at this room that was nothing like she had imagined it would be.

In her dreams, her bedroom had been something like

a fairy princess would have. One of those beds that had a pink fabric canopy, fluffy pillows, and thick carpet she wanted to wiggle her bare toes into. It had been pink and purple with fairy tale creatures painted on the ceiling, so when she lay on the floor, they'd smile down at her. And he'd be here.

He'd smile and hug her and promise that she'd never have to go back to the trailer again. He'd sit on her princess bed and sing one of those songs that made her think of angels and hope.

This wasn't a room for a long lost fairy princess. This was nothing like she imagined. This was the room for a stranger. Anyone could sleep here. A guest room. Her hand shook as she twisted the knot, tightening the ribbon on her wrist until it pinched.

She wanted a fairy princess room. It didn't matter that she was too old for fairy tales and make-believe creatures on the ceiling. She wanted that room so badly. She wanted to matter to him.

"Let's get you sorted," the woman said as she gently eased the bag free, well aware Kate was standing there with more of her childhood dreams smashed on the floor.

She felt hollow as her bag was laid on the bed and unzipped. Her clothes barely made a visible pile on the bed and her jaw began to ache while her eyes burned. She had absolutely nothing.

Even in the trailer she had something.

Kate watched, numb, as her new underpants were set in one drawer and her nightgown in another before her shirts were hung in the closet. Kate turned, staring. They looked small and poor as they hung in the closet.

"You're going to need a desk," the housekeeper said,

resting her hand on Kate's head, easing the new school backpack off. "We'll put you into the same school as the other children. Did you know that the other boys in the band have children too? There are the twins who are your age and little Shelby who is a few years younger. We'll set up a date to for all of you to meet. If there's anything else you think of needing, let me know."

Kate needed her mom. In this moment it didn't matter that she drank all the time and used all those drugs. Kate didn't care that she hadn't loved her. She needed her mom because she was familiar. Familiar was far better than this large bedroom where Kate felt smaller than small.

Staring at the bed, her fingers continued to worry the ribbon until she felt old fibers begin to tear. It was going to fall apart soon. There wasn't any more length to make another knot. Then what?

She wanted her trailer.

She wanted to go home.

She wanted to matter.

There was no trailer.

There was no home.

And she very much didn't matter.

Kate's eyes closed and the tears that had been building up fell. Nothing. She had nothing. She was nothing.

Still…she wished he were here.

Chapter 5

FUCKING HIDDEN TRIGGERS. They were like bear traps buried beneath brush. If he heard "I'm sorry" in that broken, teary voice one more time, he was going to find Jace and throw him off one of the many balconies. She had shivered through the shower, even when he cranked the heat to as hot as he could tolerate. Like a tiny statue, she had stood there as he cleaned the vomit off her. Whatever color had been in her face had bleached out, making her look like a pale, china doll. Only little bruises around her wrist from her knots had given him proof of life. No fidgeting. He had put her in his shirt and put her in his bed. As much as he wanted to join her, he hadn't.

Now she slept, curled in a protective ball but so petite she barely made a dent in the covers. "Fuck," he said as he retrieved his phone and thumbed in on. The clock said it was five twenty two. He found the right number and listened to the phone ring two times before a sleepy voice answered.

"Doyle? What's wrong?"

"I need your help, darlin'."

Claire was quiet. "Are you drunk?"

"No, though I'm wishing I was." He rubbed his finger over his eyebrow. "Some of my shit is hazy so I need some help recollecting."

"About what?"

"Kate."

"Kate who?"

Fuck. Seriously? "Jennings, Claire. Kate Jennings. Jace's daughter. Do you remember when she arrived?"

His ex-wife was quiet whether from surprise or thinking back. "Not really. Sorry. My head was all about Willow. Why?"

Because she had thrown up having sex with him and shut down on him. Maybe if Claire knew more, he'd mention it. "Never mind. I was just trying to see if I remembered something correctly. Go back to sleep."

"Are you sure you're clean?"

"Squeaky." He hung up and tossed the phone aside. "Fuck." Kate who. Seriously? When he looked back at her, her eyes were open and she was watching him. He had never seen sadder eyes than hers. Even when he had been hammered, he remembered how sad her eyes were.

Belinda Carver was the last person who should've been a parent. Next one on the list was Jace Jennings. Together they sure as hell shouldn't have been parents. That Kate had turned out the polar opposite of both of them seemed like a miracle to him. Both Beli and Jace had been selfish users. Jace hungry for success, Beli hungry for him to succeed. Not that Jace-fucking-Jennings would've brought Beli along for the ride. They had fucked and fought, drunk and fought, shot up and fucked all while the band had been trying to do something. Anything. A bunch of kids with a dream. Two things had happened at once: Belinda got knocked up and miracle upon miracles the band had been noticed.

None of them had looked back. None.

The casualty of that lay in his bed.

He was ninety-five percent sure Jace had known about Kate and had left her there with her addict mom. He hadn't exactly been surprised when the call had come about Kate. Jace had thundered about DNA tests, demanded proof, but Doyle was sure it had been an act.

Asshole.

One day.

One day Doyle was going to put his fist through his band mate's face until there was nothing left but a smear of DNA on the floor. "How do you feel?"

"Stupid."

"Kate."

She blushed and her shoulder moved beneath the bed. "Only I could ruin the best sex ever."

He gave a soft grunt. "Is that a trigger?"

"Well, bad sex wasn't." She pushed herself up and drew the covers up. The black against her fair skin was drastic and he didn't care for it at all.

He uncoiled from his chair, grabbed the edge of duvet and yanked it off the bed. Next, he flipped the sheets down, picked up Kate and plopped her in the middle of the feather cover.

"What are you–"

"Hush it." He scooped her up, grabbed his keys and carried her out of his room. Once they were up where he had found her last night, he set her down and dragged those who had passed out inside. Everyone in the upstairs room was politely told to fuck off before he threw them down the stairs. He sorted through the keys after locking the door. Kate watched from the chair he had put her on, surrounded by all kinds of crap from last night's party.

Fucking hell, they were too old to party like they were twenty. He was forty-two and had been sober since Claire had given him the choice while pregnant with Willow: get clean or get out. Sobriety had lasted longer than his marriage. He unlocked the door to the studio, locking it behind him. All their equipment was there, ready for more torture as they put together another album. If he didn't kill Jace first, which could happen.

Even without Kate factoring into it, he had a massive hate for Jace-fucking-Jennings. He couldn't even credit sober clarity. Nope, the hate had been there almost from the start.

He grabbed an acoustic guitar that was probably Carl's and went outside. The hot tub was disgusting. Someone's underwear floated while brown foam churned. He assumed it was vomit. Gross.

Doyle wished they weren't here, surrounded by the remains of all kinds of bodily functions. The bony remains of debauchery and stupidity. The sky was turning shades of pink, orange and violet. Until he had gotten clean, he hadn't truly appreciated how the sun looked coming up over the mountains. If he was around in the summer, Dani would join him on the back deck, him with a cup of coffee, her with hot chocolate and they'd just sit there, the birds chirping as they watched the sun creep up then that perfect moment when it hit the water.

Sometimes when he was on tour, Dani would set up the laptop beside her, the camera facing their view. God damn, he missed his mornings with her. Missed Willy wandering in as he fought lyrics. He missed his home. He missed his girls. Ten months of video chats and dropped calls was enough.

He was ready for home.

He set the guitar down and organized Kate to his liking, then he sat down between her spread legs and settled against her.

"Shouldn't it be the other way?"

"We need to get this bratting taken care off before it gets out of control."

"I am not a brat," she huffed.

She was. It made him grin as he tuned the guitar. If life had been a little gentler with her, she'd be one helluva bratty sub. "My hand, your ass." She sucked in her breath as her body stilled behind him. He strummed the familiar chord. The lyrics were a part of him, a piece of his daughters that he could pull out to be close to them. Their sweet voices joining in. It was their song, written when they had been little and the world was theirs for the taking. A theme song that let them know he'd hold the shit back until they could stand on their own, then he'd be there. Just be there no matter the outcome.

The last note faded away and he reached back, tangling his fingers into her hair and drawing her forward until he could see her. Silent tears tracked down her cheeks. "Get it?"

She nodded and sucked on her upper lip before she gave him her words. "Yes, Sir."

He stood up, eased behind her and watched the sun come up with her.

The slamming of the door and loud laughter woke Kate up. Not for the first time, she wondered at her brilliance of living with people. When she had gone to UBC, she had lived alone in residence, but because she was a bit anti-social, she had dared to up the game. In her second year, Kate had thrown her hat into the roommate pool. The experiment had, for a lack of better description, been an epic fail.

This one was heading the same way because even though she lived with two other girls, she didn't socialize with them. Cyanide concerts and after parties not withstanding.

Her room had no personal touches. No family pictures, no mementos, no hidden photo stashes under the bed. This room wasn't her.

She was tired of ghosting through her own life.

At least she was almost finished with her design course which meant project Katey Jay Designs was that much closer. No longer a dream. Almost tangible. She had suffered through four years of business so she knew what the hell she was doing. Business first, then design, because if it had been the other way she'd have procrastinated her ass off.

Once she was done with her jewelry design courses and the "what you know" column ticked off and she had the beginnings of Katey Jay Designs up, Kate was going to utterly abuse the "who you know" column to get people wearing her designs. People who when they wore something, flocks of wannabes said "I want that because so and so wore it." Yes, she was totally going to use her connection with Jace Jennings, the other members of the band and everyone they knew.

Because she was also never again going to find herself sitting on a gravel road as the smoldering remains of her home filled the air.

It didn't matter that she had more money than she really knew what to do with and that there was a bedroom she occasionally frequented in a big ass mansion on the hill over looking the harbor. It wasn't her. None of it was really hers. It was dumb luck.

All that DNA money from Jace already had a use. It was going to get her her dream.

So in a way Jace was doing something for her, even if he didn't know it. Or care.

Kate tried not to be bitter when it came to Jace and expectations. Sometimes it was hard, especially after moments where it was pointed out he sucked as a father.

Like undoubtedly fucking one of her roommates because Jace Jennings never said no. After all, that's how she came to be.

Holy hell, she was in a bad headspace. She drew her phone out from under her pillow, opened up a text window and typed in Doyle's name. After a brief hesitation, because she didn't want to bother him after seriously screwing up and ruining what she was forever going to refer to as Best Night Ever, caps included, she typed a short message.

I think I'm bottoming out.

The phone rang almost instantly making her jump. "Hi."

"You think or you are?"

"Am." She drew her knees up and wrapped her free arm around. "Does it take this long? I just woke up from a nap and I'm all…" She shrugged.

"Use your words, Katey." As if he knew.

"I know I'm a disaster, I get that, but it's like it's pressing down on me."

"Tell me what's pressing on you." His voice was low and calm making tears burn. If anything he should be pissed. Who ruined sex like that?

My life.

She swallowed, her elbow now on her knee so she could rest her head in her palm.

"Is this about what happened?"

"Yes. No. Maybe. No."

"Pick a word, Kate."

She sighed. "Yes."

"What did I tell you I'd do if we hit a trigger? Or it didn't feel right?"

"Stop," she whispered as she closed her eyes.

"There will never be a point of no return with me, Kate. I'm forty-two, not sixteen. I knew that with you we were going to hit a lot of dark moments, because a lot has happened to you. Stuff I know, stuff you haven't shared yet. I guess that's why I was a dick with you at the club, because shit comes out and you've been tossed around enough. I can control the bruises on your body, but I can't control the internal ones. So we stop, figure it out, then work through it."

She wiped the heel of her hand down her cheek. "Really? Why? There's got to be someone less damaged than me. Someone better at this."

"It's not like there are report cards, Kate. You don't get graded. Now, because I'm learning you're very good at evading, what's pressing down on you? Tell me."

Kate sighed, suddenly exhausted from everything.

"I'm so tired of being me, Doyle."

"Why? I'm discovering Katey Jay is a lot more interesting than she gives herself credit for. Get some rest. And Kate? You *will* tell me. Maybe not today, but you will."

"Why?"

"Because that's what trust is all about. The day you realize you can trust me is gonna be a fantastic fucking day. Maybe even a day of fantastic fucking. No maybe about it. I already know what it's like to be inside you. Fantastic is a given. This isn't instantaneous. There's no magic wand to be waved. Trust doesn't appear with a great orgasm. It doesn't even come with being topped. It just comes. Like the sunrise we watched this morning, it just rises up and there it is. Time and patience, girl. Time and patience."

"You're pretty poetic for a rock and roll bad ass."

"Baby, you ain't seen nothing yet. Better?"

She nodded and smiled at his slow sigh. She gave him her words. "Yes, Sir."

"That's hot. That's so fucking hot." He disconnected in the middle of the giggle that bubbled out.

She pressed her phone against her head. "It just rises up and there it is," she whispered. She looked around her dull, impersonal bedroom, then climbed out of bed. First a shower and then she was going to go give herself a sunrise.

She was going shopping.

Kate – 2002

Her name was Shaelynn Darby and she hated Kate. She saw it in the woman's eyes. Shaelynn was pretty. She was probably the prettiest woman Kate had ever seen. She had beautiful blonde hair that rippled down her back in waves. This wasn't the same peroxide blonde Mom would have done for a couple of dollars in one of the ladies' trailers, it was something else entirely different. She was tanned, tall and thin – very much everything Mom hadn't been. She also looked as if she had swallowed a basketball. She was having Jace's baby. Kate's brother or sister.

"So this is it." In a crisp voice, she ordered, "Come with me," and led the way over the smooth black floor. Her high heels made sharps sounds, like a gun firing bullets. Kate followed her up the curved staircase to the top floor of the house. The white carpet was thick beneath her bare feet and that's why she had been walking around without shoes or socks. The novelty of the plush carpet and smooth floor tiles made her feel safe for some reason. Nothing was rotting beneath Kate's feet. There were no unknown stains on peeling linoleum. While she felt really small and alone in Jace Jennings' house, she still felt far safer here then in the trailer.

Shaelynn entered Jace's bedroom like she owned not just the room but also the house. The room was in back and white: white carpet, glossy black furniture, white walls, and black sheets. All of the house was like this as if nobody liked color. Shaelynn tossed her purse onto the shiny dresser and dropped a paper bag in the middle of the floor.

"There are rules here," she said as she let her jacket fall to the floor, not seeming to care about the mess she was Shaelynn. "You will not bother me or Jace. When the baby comes, you will not bother her. Jace didn't have to take you in. I highly doubt you're really his. He did it because of the slut, Belinda." She walked into a closet almost as big as Kate's bedroom. Kate didn't follow.

"We'll feed and clothe you." The woman poked her head out the closet and gave Kate a look that said she found her disgusting. "Because it is expected, but make no mistake that you are a guest here."

"Are you married to Jace?"

Shaelynn's eyes narrowed to little blue slits and her mouth went tight. Suddenly she wasn't so pretty. "I don't want anything to do with you. Do not embarrass us and that means calling Jace Dad or Father. We both know he's not. You can go now." She waved her hand like Kate was a fly buzzing about her.

Back in her room, Kate shut the door. Her hand slid along the large bed, the sheets cool. She had made her bed this morning, but someone had come in to do a better job of it. The pillows looked fluffier as they formed a soft looking mountain against the headboard. She still hadn't seen Jace.

Glancing at the door, on the off chance someone suddenly opened it, Kate counted to three. After she grabbed one of the pretty little pillows, she eased under the bed. The carpet was so soft and it smelled clean. A far cry from that moldy, stuffy air in her hiding spot in the trailer. She didn't have any pictures of him. Yet.

Tucking the pillow under her cheek, she folded her arms beneath it. Kate was surprised to realize she missed Mom. It was darker under the bed and the enclosed area made her feel not so small and insignificant. The silence wrapped around her as she thought over Shaelynn's words.

Jace *was* her dad, no matter what Shaelynn said. There was proof. All those tests had said so. Kate tried to imagine calling him Dad. To his face. Or someone else.

It didn't feel right. Not like Mom did. Maybe because that's what she had called her all her life, that's who she was. Jace Jennings was…well…

He was Jace Jennings.

Kate stared at the wall. She needed some pictures of him. This space didn't feel like hers without pictures. Shifting, her foot bumped a can taken from the massive pantry. All that food. She shifted to fix it so no one saw it. Once again, she settled into place.

Shaelynn yelled for Mrs. Dawson, the housekeeper, to "clean up this shit." Take away her pretty clothes and all of Jace's money and Kate knew exactly who she was.

She was just like Mom.

Giving her that identity made Kate not so scared of her. After all, the odds of her going hungry in this house were pretty slim, she rolled over to double-check on the cans of food and decided maybe one more, just in case.

She woke up to the door opening and she turned her head to watch the feet move. The shoes weren't those clean white ones Mrs. Dawson wore or the heels Shaelynn wore. These were heavy looking boots with chains going from the ankle and under the sole. Jace!

Jace was in the room. Unsure of what to do, Kate pressed her face into her pillow. She didn't want to get caught under the bed but she really wanted to see him. There was a soft thump before he turned and walked out. Curious to the sound, she crawled out and looked around. On the bed was a thick envelope.

She opened it and stared at the collection of red and

brown bills. Her eyes went wide as she sat on the floor and began to count out the money. Fifties and hundreds. Bills she had never seen beyond math books in school. When she was done, she stared. There was two thousand dollars.

She had two thousand dollars.

Two.

Thousand.

Dollars.

It was more money than she'd ever held in her life and she had no idea what to do with it. If she was with Mom some would go for rent, but most would go up Mom's nose. But Mom wasn't here. This was *her* money. Putting all the bills carefully in place, she returned to her spot under the bed, and Kate tucked the envelope under the box spring. Jace was home.

That thought dragged her from her sanctuary and she ran down the stairs, almost slipping on the glossy white tiles. She had no idea where to go now that she was on the main level. A lot of the house was still strange to her.

Fortunately, she didn't have to go looking too hard.

Unfortunately, he was fighting. With Shaelynn.

And it was all about Kate.

Chapter 6

THE FIRST PERSON Doyle saw upon waking was his ex-wife. That was one way of killing his morning wood. With a sigh, he flung the sheets aside and climbed out of bed naked. Ignoring her, he went to take a shower. His shower. God, he missed his shower.

"Fuck me," he muttered as Claire followed him in and leaned against the sink, her arms folded over her chest. "In case you missed it, we've been divorced for eight years. I don't have to deal with evil eyes in my shower. Fuck off. Go make coffee."

"In case you missed it," she snapped back, "we've been divorced for eight years. Make your own fucking coffee."

He grunted as he tilted his face into the spray.

"Kate Jennings, Doyle."

"Coffee, Claire."

"You're not the boss of me anymore, Kolemann." She flipped her middle finger but left him to his shower. Probably a good thing since Kate's name made him think of Kate naked in his bed and hello erection. No, Kate on the balcony. That moment her fingers dipped between her legs as she obeyed. Without hesitation. Instantly lost in the moment. Fuck, that moment. It was a beautiful thing.

He hadn't lied to her. He wouldn't. One of his favorite masturbations was to a sub surrendering. If for the past year she had green eyes, well, so be it, but now he knew how she looked, how she felt. How she moaned *"Yes, Sir."*

"Fuck." His stomach muscles contracted as his hand fisted around his dick, cum streaming forth. Exhaling, he let the warm water hit the back of his neck, working muscles that had been tense ever since it had gone tits up. A woman didn't freak out during sex because her parents were negligent asshole addicts. That came from sexual abuse or rape. "Fuck."

The thought of someone hurting her like that…

How much? How much did she have to take?

Her *"I'm so tired of being me"* had chased him into his dreams, mind-fucking him and making him jerk awake at odd times throughout the night.

If Jace knew or was responsible, Doyle was going to fucking kill him.

Knuckles rapped on the shower door and he looked at his ex-wife and ex-sub. "Coffee. You look like you need it."

He needed it with a shot of Irish. Pushing open the door, he turned off the water, stepped out and took the peace offering. He drank first then dried off, wandering into his closet for a pair of jeans and a shirt from one of the events at the girls' school. Despite the seclusion of his home, he wasn't much of a rock star here. He had the small music studio tucked behind the house but that was about it. Hell, even his toy bag didn't come here. Who would he use it on? Claire? That bridge had been burned a long time ago. Plus the girls were always coming and going. That's all he needed.

Here he got to be Doyle Kolemann, just like it said on his property bill and birth certificate.

Pushing open the double doors to his bedroom, he stepped out onto the wood deck that gave him an amazing view of the Strait of Georgia. Bracing his arms on the railing, he looked down to the rocky beach where he could see the girls. Home.

Claire settled beside him, also watching those two beautiful lives they created. "You look tired, Doyle."

"Ten months of hotels, buses, planes and Jace-fucking-Jennings are enough to exhaust me. Fuck being tired, doll."

"You hate it so much. Why not leave?"

"And what, Claire?" Dani's laugh drifted up to them. It came from the belly and always made him grin. How the hell had he made up half of those two girly-girls? "Find a new band? How many are here? So I what? Relocate? See the girls sporadically because we both know you wouldn't follow. This is home. I'm too old to start over again. I love what I do. I just hate that fucker so bad."

She was quiet, well aware of his feelings toward his band mate. "You miss so much on tour, Doyle. They miss you so much. Willow's talking about dating."

"Fuck that. She's twelve. No boys for ten years. Minimum." Dating? Jesus. He was not ready for that. Funny how that hadn't come up in all their chats. Retirement. He was forty-two. Yeah, he had enough money he never needed to work again even while giving Claire enough alimony and child support that she didn't need to work. Even cracked out of his head, he had been meticulous about his earnings. Investments and business deals to fatten the account. He had been poor. He wasn't going to do it again. His daughters weren't going to go through that either. But what would he do? His last hobby had put him in the hospital with a stomach pump and a defibrillator and his wife threatening to walk away with his kid.

"Kate Jennings," Claire said quietly. "Seriously, Doyle? She's what? Twenty?"

His eyebrows rose as he looked at her. "Seriously? We're playing the age card? She's twenty-four. You know that. Over the halfway mark, which puts her out of mid-life crisis zone."

She snorted into her mug. "You're such an asshole."

He grinned and looked away. "I hit a trigger with her and it was bad. It was really fucking bad, Claire."

She rubbed his back and rested her head against his shoulder. "You're good with those. Be careful with this though."

"Do you really think Jace will give a fuck? Now? Caring isn't one of his strengths."

"You're being an asshole, Kolemann."

He was. Jace didn't factor into this. "I'm going to hurt that girl, Claire. She's…fragile."

"That's part of the process sometimes. She's survived Belinda and Jace. She's tougher than you're giving her credit for."

He looked at his ex. Her strawberry blonde hair was in a new pixie cut and her blue eyes filled with a joy and contentment that he had never been able to put there. He had tried. She had tried. His pretty girl. That joy and contentment came from the ring on her finger, from a man who didn't have to try. "You subs are like that."

She grinned and her dimples appeared. "You know it."

"Brat." Her eyebrows rose as she sipped her coffee, looking all innocent. "Have you talked to Daisy lately?"

"No. Why?"

"Daaaaaaad!"

Doyle finished his coffee. "Call Daisy, Claire. It's seven in the morning, keep it down," he shouted at Dani. Even from his vantage point he could see her smile. She waved and returned to checking out the tide pools. Claire rubbed his back, then left him. He looked over his shoulder, staring at his cell and with a muttered curse, he opened up a text window. *You good?*

Seven, came the response. *Seven.*

DOYLE: *I warned you about the bratting.*

KATE: Zzz.

DOYLE: *Are you good, Kate?*

KATE: Yes, Sir.

Fuck. Even in text it got to him. He shoved his phone into his back pocket. He ditched his mug for a pair of worn sneakers, then went out to join his daughters. Willy grinned at him, flashing new metal over her teeth. "So, are you able to go through airport security with all that?"

"Daaad." She rolled her eyes even as she giggled. She grabbed his hand and swung their arms and he admitted that he liked that even at the wise age of twelve she still did that. "Are we still going to work on my song?"

"Yep. Mind the dead jellyfish," he said, deadpan. She shrieked, jumped and hit him as she saw there was nothing there. "Just testing." She had been Dani's age when she hadn't minded his warning and stepped on a dead jellyfish. There was no coming back from that. It was, they had decided a year later, better than when she had slipped in the mud and landed on a rotting trout corpse that some bear had passed on. "I thought about what you asked, Will, and I'm going to pass."

"But—"

"If I judge the contest, honey, you can't enter. I'd rather you enter." Last night she had pitched him to be a judge in a songwriting contest that had just opened up an under eighteen category. He watched her consider that, then she nodded.

"I'd rather I entered too."

Hooking an arm around her neck, he kissed the top of her head. The German shepherd mix who had decided that both his and Claire's homes were also his came out of the trees and raced toward them. He gave a happy bark as he discovered a beached log and decided that was his new stick.

When his marriage had finally gasped its last breath before dying, and after the hot flash of anger had faded, they had sat down to decide what was best not just for the girls but for all four of them. He loved his three girls. They had, in that magic way love did, changed his life. It wasn't just him being sober but that empty core inside him had been filled. First by Claire, then Willow and finally Danielle. Not being a part of their life had terrified him. Nightmares of pills and overdoses had haunted him.

After the dust had settled, this was the solution. Claire had gotten the house and he had built on the land next door. There was a well-worn path marching from her place to his where the kids traveled whenever they wanted when he was home. No paperwork saying only weekends. If they wanted to be at his place, they were at his place. Sometimes one, sometimes both. His divorce was better than his marriage. Hell, he had walked Claire down the aisle when she had remarried. Claire would always be his family because of Willy and Dani. Somewhere along the way, his ex-wife had transformed into his best friend. Go fucking figure.

Only one marriage out of the band had lasted and that was saying something. There were messed up kids everywhere who became secondary. The moment he had held a weird looking alien baby in his hands the job had become secondary. Ironic since he had been so hungry for fame and money, the music a catalyst for a lot of the shit in his life. Despite what he had said to Claire, if he had to pick, he'd ditch Cyanide faster than hell.

"You'll come over tonight?" Willow asked.

He nodded and they both watched Scamp find a smaller stick, what looked like a sapling, carrying it along the beach all proud and shit. A second hand slid into his and he looked down at Dani. "Hey, baby."

A happy sigh came from her as she rested her head against his arm. It was an amazing thing to realize he wasn't fucking up his kids. They weren't overly spoiled, they weren't in the eye of a camera, they weren't putting shit up their nose because their old man did and they weren't looking at the world with sad eyes. Not bad for an asshole like him. Not bad at all.

Chin resting on her bent knee, Kate stared at the sketch pad that had nothing on it. Her finger flicked the drum stick back and forth. Yesterday's shopping spree at her favorite flea market had landed her a violin case, an old acoustic guitar, and a bag of assorted scrap. The bag had been a gold mine. A collection of guitar picks that were broken, a piano key, a drum stick, a broken guitar string. Oh the beauties that had been bagged up for her, salvaged from things that wouldn't normally sell. She was currently lusting over an old piano and was trying to justify the cost and adding it to her inventory. She already had two pianos in various states of disembowelment. Did she need a third?

You betcha.

But her loft was getting crowded, so denying herself the piano made her heart ache just a smidge. The loft was hers. The minute she had seen it, she had lusted. It had been the high ceilings because that meant high walls. High walls meant storage. One wall was made up of custom shelves that held small items from all kinds of strings to wind instruments to salvaged items off instruments. It had given her a total rush when she had begun to fill them. Instruments in various stages of dismemberment were on the walls like artwork. A gutted cello, her guitar collection. Her two pianos were equally gutted. Heck, she even had a drum kit she had found for cheap at a garage sale. Hanging between her massive track lighting system were all kinds of bows from stringed instruments. Her rolling safety ladder got a hard workout some days.

Thanks to Cyanide's manager, she had an endless supply of guitar picks, broken guitar and bass strings, and black drum sticks that had been broken or worn down. She had the broken guitar from when Jace had been drunk and smashed it. She had all the old, dead amplifiers and even a cymbal from Doyle's drum kit because he hadn't liked its sound. If the band was given free instruments or accessories they didn't like, they were in her inventory.

The majority of her jewelry contained some musical instrument. It had started all by chance, her jewelry designing. Her knotted bracelet had been her first and pretty much only thing that didn't have music associated with it. She had found a guitar string lying around and she had begun to play with it. That guitar string had snowballed into her loft.

The black ring on Doyle's thumb? Hers. She had found herself staring at an ebony piano key a year ago. Since she couldn't carve worth a damn and the key was narrow, she had found a carver to do the work for her. Two angled lines in a wide based vee so the skin showed and the inside had to be rounded to fit the thumb. That had been the hardest because when had she ever touched his thumb to make sure the wood would rest perfectly? She hadn't.

Luck and skill. Once the ring was put together, and it just looked right to her, she had tucked it into a small ring box and with his name on a blank card, she had left it at the club. Risky. Foolish. When she next saw him he had been wearing it.

A piece of her was on him.

She should tell him. Actually, she *wanted* to tell him.

Pressing the tip of her finger against the drum stick, she set it rolling across her floor before she impulsively reached for her phone. *I have a secret*, she texted him.

His response came a few minutes later. *Only one?*

Many. But I'm only going to give one. She retrieved the drum stick and ran her thumb over the tip, studying the edge then down the narrow neck. Beside her the phone chirped a few times. Pressing her thumb against the pale wood, she shut one eye as she looked at a child's ukulele on the wall. "Well, hi," she said as she picked up her pencil, frowning at her phone when it nagged her again.

DOYLE: *Kate.*

KATE: Second. I gotta do this before it's gone.

DOYLE: *What?*

DOYLE: *Kate.*

DOYLE: *Kate.*

She bent over the sketchbook and put the piece down before it was gone. Not that it would disappear, but yeah. Once it was in her head, it was there, but now… now it was tangible. "Fun," she said as she looked at the drawing. The cherry red of the ukulele's sound hole with the tip of the drum stick dangling in the middle. Fishing wire, she thought, so it looked invisible. She'd keep the chipped paint surrounding the sound hole because it had musical notes and she'd carve on onto the drum stick. The nylon strings braided to make up the chain for the oversized necklace. "Jamboree." Not done. She drew a fine line at the bottom followed by a musical note that would sparkle there. Red? Oh yeah, red.

Smiling she tapped the drum stick on the floor and picked up her phone. *Sorry. That was rude.*

DOYLE: *Hm.*

KATE: Do you still want the secret?

DOYLE: *If it's that you brat, not really a secret.*

That made her grin. *I don't brat. Do I?*

DOYLE: *My hand. Your ass. That's what bratting gets you.*

A shiver moved down her spine and she flattened her hand on her stomach. *You keep saying that and yet…*

DOYLE: *My hand. Your ass. Tell me.*

Kate exhaled and realized she was nervous. Really nervous. *You know that ring on your left thumb? I gave that to you.*

She shook out her hands and hunched over her phone. *I made it.*

DOYLE: *I know.*

KATE: What? How… You know?

DOYLE: *Now I have a secret.*

Kate stuck her tongue out at the phone and went to retrieve the ukulele. In the bedroom upstairs she had all her heavy-duty machinery. A band saw was against the wall, while a lathe was along the other, and a table saw sat in the middle of the room. Just your normal loft decor.

Really, she probably should've found an industrial workspace, but here she had a view out the large windows of the harbor. The space didn't feel like a shop class. It felt like a studio. And it was hers. While there were no pictures of her family and she was no longer hoarding images of Jace, this space had Kate Jace Jennings all over it. Her bedrooms at the apartment and the mansion were just for sleeping in. This was where she lived.

She pulled on her work apron and grabbed her safety glasses. Her phone was set on the low wall that opened up the workshop to the loft, music playing from it. Not Cyanide. Sitting on her stool, she unstrung the ukulele and set the small tuning pegs in a little bucket to be added to the storage shelves. Next she took the ukulele to the table saw, adjusted everything and with a small prayer to the machine gods that she didn't cut off anything that needed to stay attached, mostly to her, she neatly sliced off the front of child's instrument.

Next she dug out a compass, marked her cut line plus her destination line and slowly cut the circle out. Sitting on the floor, with music filling the space with happy beats, she began to sand. Forget meditation, this was her zen. When the light began to fade from the windows, she finally turned on her lights and returned to smoothing the wood. She loved it when the circle became a true circle, when the broken edges were gone. Finally no marker remained and she blew off the wood dust. She turned it around to see the hand painted musical notes frame the inner circle. In some places the gold notes were faded, perhaps where the heel of a small hand had rested. Resting her elbows on her bent knees, the smell of sawdust tickling her nose, Kate felt at one with the world.

This was where she belonged. Here there were no doubts, no insecurities. No one judged her. No addict mother haunted the corners here, no uncaring father, no snotty half-sisters. It was just Kate and her dream. She picked up her phone and opened up the chat she had going with Doyle.

Remember how I asked you to tell me what world I belonged in since you said I didn't belong in Edge?

It took a few minutes for him to respond. But his *yes* was blunt.

KATE: *And how I said I was tired of being me?*
DOYLE: *Yes.*
KATE: *Do you want to see my world?*
DOYLE: *Yes.*

She snapped a picture of her workshop and sent it to him. *Sometimes I forget not everything is shitty and that I do have a place in the world. Maybe it's not the Cyanide world and it's not Mom's world. But this…this is Kate's world. Do you want to see more?*

DOYLE: *Yes.*

She cleared her throat as she stood up. Bracing her elbows on the wall she turned on the video function and scanned the camera over her wall of guitars, violins, cellos and everything else in between. Some were whole, some looked like her ukulele, some were just the sides, some just the front. There was her drafting table that let her see the water, the work table that was a disaster of all the things she had on the go. She leaned over the half wall where she had oh so meticulously painted her logo. Katey Jay Designs. The K and J entwined and a musical note was hooked over the curve of the J.

No one. She had showed no one. Who would she show? Who would she possibly share this with? A man who didn't care about her? A man who had pretty much ignored her existence for twenty-four years? The same man who had broken her heart year after year after year. She exhaled sharply, turned the phone around and stopped recording. She hit send and continued to look down at her dream.

Her dream. The phone rang.

"Katey." His voice was soft and she dropped her head into her hand. Tears slid unchecked, plopping onto the wood.

"I'm going to use him, Doyle. I'm going to use his celebrity and his name. I'm going to use the fact that I'm the daughter of Jace Jennings. When I'm done school, I'm going to open a store on one of the trendy streets and then I'm going to remind the world that thirteen years ago Kate Jace Jennings was the long lost daughter of Jace Jennings because if the only thing I have of his, is his name, then, by fucking God, I'm going to use it."

"Good. I want you to remember this moment, Katey Jay."

"Why?"

"Because this is the moment where you just owned yourself. Because this is the moment where you started to trust me. You know, this morning Claire said you're tougher than I give you credit for. But pay attention, you're even tougher than you give yourself credit for."

"Yeah?" In the background she heard a girl shout for Dad. "You gotta go."

"She's twelve. She needs to learn patience at some time. Remember this moment, Katey Jay."

"Yes, Sir."

"Jesus. I'm hanging with my kid, girl."

She smiled as she hung up. Wiping her cheeks, she looked out at the loft. "This moment. It's a sunrise moment."

Kate - 2002

Kate had never been to a school like her new one. She hadn't liked her blue uniform with the school patch on the pocket of her blazer. Not until she had realized that *everyone* was wearing the same thing. Unlike her old school when she had shown up in used clothes, no one at her new school knew she had lived in a trailer starting to rot with a mother who was also rotting. She had looked like everyone else. The teacher had introduced her to her class, told her to sit in an empty desk and so had begun her day.

She had been terrified about her first day in a new

school. Not that she had a lot of friends at her old school, but there had been comfort in the familiar. She had barely slept and instead had roamed the house, learning her way around. In the morning a man wearing a black suit had rung the doorbell and driven her to her new school. No one had wished her good luck or even saw her leave but that had been familiar.

Lunch had been provided so she hadn't been hungry. She had even made a few friends, which in itself was amazing. At her old school she had stuck out and not in a good way, so friends had been pretty rare for her. Plus, it wasn't like she could invite anyone over since who knew if Mom was sober or alone? Even though she had craved the company of others, she hadn't sought them out. But now…now she looked like she belonged. Her uniform was her new favorite thing.

Shutting the door behind her, she winced at the echoing bang it made. Even now she expected Mom to yell at her to not make so much noise. No one yelled.

She took off her shiny new shoes and set them in the closet and took her new bag up to her room. The new desk that Mrs. Dawson had magically made appear was ready for her to work on. It was a lot prettier than the battered table she had worked on before. No wobbling. No weird stains. She couldn't wait to use it. She had resisted the call of the glossy white paint, patiently waiting to use it as it was meant to be used. She changed out of her uniform, setting it in the hamper Mrs. Dawson had told her to put it in. She had two uniforms, one to wear while the other was being dry cleaned. Dry cleaned!

Kate changed into a pair of jeans and a t-shirt, pulling out her books, determined to prove that she wasn't as useless as Shaelynn said she was. Kate did her homework, swinging her feet as she hummed. No one was there to tell her not to.

Sometimes she missed Mom, but mostly it was a relief to not be screwing up all the time. No bottles were thrown at her, there was always food, and she didn't wake up scared.

She lost track of time as she completed all her homework and even started to read a book for one of her classes, so when her stomach growled at her, she was a bit surprised. She left the quiet of her room and found herself standing there, listening to the quiet of the house.

It was a weird quiet. Usually Shaelynn was complaining about something or yelling at Mrs. Dawson. No dinner smells drifted up. The house felt different. Holding her breath, she walked down the stairs and saw the kitchen was empty. The large glass table wasn't set, the television or stereo weren't on. Her stomach started to hurt as she walked down the curving stairs into the basement.

The faint sickly sweet smell that seemed to cling to the room was still there but no one was on the round sectional couch, no smoke drifted up to the ceiling. She walked to the room that she wasn't allowed in and knocked quietly on the door, wondering if Jace was inside. The door was locked.

She folded her arms over her chest and began to search every room in the house on every floor. There was no one here.

Her stomach wasn't growling from hunger so much as it was from nerves. Her heart was beating so fast against her ribs, her chest actually hurt. In Jace's office, she looked for a clue. He didn't really use the office, his personal assistant did, so it was neatly organized, but there was no clue as to where everyone was.

All she knew was that they weren't here.

No one appeared when she got ready for bed. The house was still unnaturally empty when she crawled out from under her bed, needing the comfort of her private hiding place. She sat on one of the stiff leather couches wearing her new uniform and stared at one of the weird paintings. She should eat, because her head felt funny and she felt a little nauseous. She had missed enough meals in her life to know what was wrong.

The doorbell rang and it seemed to echo around her, bouncing off the floors and walls. Kate picked up her bag and tried to breathe past the tightness in her throat. Her eyes burned as she opened the door to see the driver from yesterday.

"Good morning, Miss Jennings."

She wanted to fling herself at the man. She locked the door and followed him to the shiny black car sitting in the drive.

"Are you ready for another day of learning?"

She nodded as she slid into the back seat. She missed her mom. At least she had never forgotten her. Yes, she had spent a lot of time alone when Mom had decided she was old enough to look after herself, but she had always been there in the morning. Maybe passed out or drunk or high, but she was always there. She felt small and scared again. Like when Mom had died and she realized she was alone. Utterly alone.

She bent her head as the tears began to slide free. She was so tired of feeling alone and forgotten. She was just a kid. It was supposed to be different here. Reality had shown her otherwise but she still wished it were different. She wished Jace wanted her around. She wished he loved her. She wished she could call him Dad. She wished that this was like all her dreams. She wished. She always wished. She wanted life to be different. She wanted Mom back.

Always wanting.

Chapter 7

AS THE FIRE sparked up into the night, Doyle tapped his phone that sat on the arm of the Adirondack chair. The warm weight of Dani sleeping against his chest was almost as good as it got.

"Claire thinks I should be worried about you. Pardon me. Concerned." Oz Peters flicked quote marks with his fingers around the word. "I told her you were now a legal adult and could make your own decisions."

"How'd that go over?"

Oz slanted a look at him, sipping his beer. "So consider me concerned."

"This," Doyle made air quotes, "totally gives you credibility."

"I know. I also know you've been staring at that phone for about fifteen minutes. Unless you get your ass moving, you'll miss the last ferry. You also have this ridiculously amazing friend who can zip you across the strait lickety split. Faster, then say, a ferry."

"Ridiculously awesome friends don't say lickety split."

"They do when there's a minor in the room. Last time we talked, there was all this "she's not my girl" vomiting from you after you scared her out of my club."

"Maybe it's someone else."

"Maybe I have erectile dysfunction. Considering I make my wife's eyes roll back – well."

"That's the mother of my children you're talking about."

"Like a slot machine. Ping ping."

"Jesus, Oz." Doyle shook his head.

"Cashes out every time."

"Minor in the room."

"Please, she sleeps like the dead. I used to put a mirror under her nose to see if she was breathing."

Doyle nodded. He had too. He smoothed his hand down Dani's hair and adjusted the blanket they were bundled under.

Oz tapped his middle finger against the neck of the bottle. "You watch her. Before you approach, you watch her watching everything. I didn't really notice her when she first joined. Pretty sub with careful eyes. There are a few, but I began to notice her because of you. Every time she's in, she perches on the railing and watches with this palpable need to be in the pit. But if she's approached she says no and watches. Then you came in." Oz snapped his fingers. "It's like she came online. Sure she fled like her ass was on fire, but zap. Awake. And you, my friend. You play. You find a willing girl but you don't keep them. I bet you wouldn't even recognize them if they were standing before you now."

"Wow. Your opinion of me is stellar."

"Don't be an asshole." Oz set his bottle down and leaned forward in his chair, staring at Doyle. "It's all consensual and good dirty fun, but her. Her you see. Did you come in the other night looking for her?"

Doyle shook his head as he ran his index finger over the ring. "No."

"You sure? Because you found her pretty fast. I watch, I observe. I've known you a long time, D. Am I wrong?"

"I'm not talking about this with my kid here."

"Done." Oz uncoiled from his chair, scooped up Dani and carried her inside.

"Damn it." Leaning down, he grabbed a log and threw it in the pit, sending a shower of red sparks into the night. Bracing his elbows on his knees, he spun the ring around. He didn't want to talk about this. At least Claire knew some of Kate's history. He wasn't about to dump her past in the lap of someone she didn't know.

Grabbing his phone, he abandoned his chair and headed home. Instead of going into his house, he found himself veering down to the beach. He sat on driftwood that had escaped the logging industry and opened up the video Kate had sent him. What got him was how the image began to shake when she showed her logo and the sound of her shaky breaths that told him just how big that moment had been for her.

"Seriously, D. If we take the bird, I can get you to the mainland in under thirty minutes."

"Jesus. You're like a terrier. I just got home. The girls…"

"Have school tomorrow. They won't miss you. A car can pick you up at the flight center and take you anywhere."

The penthouse was two blocks away from where Oz landed his plane. His friend sat down beside him and picked up some rocks before throwing them into the water. "You think I don't get it? The need to connect with her? I was on the opposite side of that water wanting to be over here with Claire. It's the ultimate mind-fuck, the early stages, because you have no fucking idea what's going on. So," Oz grabbed Doyle's phone and because the window hadn't locked him out, he had access. He blocked with his elbow when Doyle tried to snatch it back. "Twenty minutes." He hit send then handed the phone back.

"You said thirty."

"Heh. I'm an asshole."

Doyle watched a response text pop up. *What happens in twenty minutes?*

Penthouse happens in twenty minutes. "You're beyond an asshole."

"Dude, I'm family. You're about to leave your subbie standing around if you don't get up off your ass."

Her *Yes, Sir* had him moving just a little bit faster while Oz's laughter followed him into the house to grab his keys and wallet.

Kate's heart slammed up into her chest when the elevator doors opened and Doyle leaned against the far wall, his tattoo-covered hands resting on the railing and his ankles crossed. He pushed himself away and reached over to the side.

"We can stay here or go to Edge. This is your call, Katey. What do you want?"

She rubbed a knot and stopped when a dark eyebrow rose. "Edge," she answered in a low voice. He nodded and stepped out. The doors stayed open.

"I need to grab my kit."

She followed him to the door and watched him enter a long code into a recessed panel as he unlocked the door. Without the penthouse crawling with people, it seemed a little eerie. He unlocked the door to his suite and she watched as he grabbed the back of his t-shirt while he entered the walk-in closet. She stood and watched him pull on a simple black shirt, exchanging the old jeans that held the faint scent of wood smoke for a pair of black jeans. He grabbed a black bag and her stomach went jittery at the sight. All kind of evil dom-y things were in that bag.

"Doyle?" She fidgeted with her bracelet and he nodded.

"Sit on the bed, I have to send the elevator down and lock the door."

Exhaling slowly, she went and sat on the bed, her hands smoothing over the cushiony duvet. Within minutes he was back and her gaze locked on the bag he set down at the foot of the bed. The clink of metal made her heart race. She watched him walk alongside of the bed then stand between her legs. The man looked massively huge.

He ran his thumb down her cheek and her skin went warm at the contact. The room felt still in the silence. "We're going to go a little slower tonight. I catapulted you into this the other night and you're cautious by nature. Okay?"

She nodded and he simply looked at her, waiting. "Okay."

"Why'd you run the first time we bumped into each other?"

Well, that was unexpected. His thumb traced her

lower lip and her skin tingled in response. "Truth?"

"Always."

"I was shocked, embarrassed."

"Why? Never be embarrassed about who you are and what you need. I probably wouldn't have flipped my shit on you if you hadn't fled like I was the bogey-man."

"You were an ass after."

He nodded. "I was. You still ran though."

The room felt warm as he gazed down at her, his thoughts hidden. "I didn't run at the party."

"You wanted to."

Only because he was really overwhelming. Scary because of all the tangled things he made her feel.

"Stand up on the bed."

Her eyebrows rose but she did as he asked, giving her the unusual benefit of looking down at him. His finger hooked in the neck of the t-shirt she had hastily thrown on when she had received his text. His other hand fisted in her hair and her stomach jerked at the sensation. He guided her head down toward his and he stopped her with a few centimeters separating them.

As she stared into the inky darkness of his eyes, she gripped the shoulder seams of his shirt.

"Why did you change your mind?" His gaze moved over her face.

"Because I'm scared of a repeat of the other night and the club is safe and neutral, only everyone would see. But if it goes great, everyone would see and I don't want to share that moment with a room filled with strangers."

"I need you to be very honest with your answers right now, Katey Jay, because they're going to determine how this goes from here on out. That trip-wire I triggered came at a pretty pivotal moment. Were you raped?"

Her heart froze and her fingers spasmed. He rested his head against hers. "Are we stopping? Doyle?" Oh God, if this was stopping, she wasn't entirely sure she could survive another failed moment. Because that would mean she was an utter failure at something she really, really wanted.

"No." His voice was low and rough. "But I need a minute." His arm hooked beneath her ass and he lifted her off the bed. The balcony door whispered open and a cool breeze drifted in. He lowered her, her body sliding down his. When her feet touched down, he turned her.

This was stopping. Her fingers fumbled over her bracelet as she stared blankly at the water. Always wanting. "It doesn't define me, you know. I went to some support groups in university, after that bad sex I told you about, and…"

"Kate. What did I tell you on this very balcony the other night? I take this very seriously and I am going to handle any and all of your triggers just as seriously. Did you not say that what really pushed your button was the prep?"

She nodded.

"The prep isn't about laying out the toys or picking what piece of naughty furniture to tie you to. It happens long before we step into the pit. It starts here." His finger stroked along her temple and her eyes closed at the simple touch. "A touch, whether it's my skin against yours or my gaze meeting yours. It is that first connection. It is that moment where you realize that I see you, I see what breathes deep in your soul."

She shivered as his fingers caressed the side of her

face, down her throat. Her head rested against his chest and he took her hand and rested it on the railing.

"Long before I put you on that cross, and make no mistake, girl, I want you on that cross, I'm going to let you know that every beautiful inch of you is safe beneath my touch. Gentle." His fingers feathered over the base of her throat and heat moved through her body. "Or hard." She sucked in her breath when he pushed on the knot resting against the soft flesh of her wrist. "Take it in," he coaxed as his hand slid over her breast, the touch at total odds with the pain. "You have no idea how much I like this bracelet."

The pressure eased and she found herself breathing heavily, her body well aware of what he could do with five little knots.

"Just like that," he whispered against her ear. "Feel." He lifted her hand and rested it over her other breast. Through the thin lace of her bra her nipple was hard, aching at the contact. His thumb feathered back and forth over her wrist as he caressed up her neck, tilting her head back. "My domination isn't in the crop that I would flick over your nipples and clit or snap against your breasts, stomach, thighs and pussy. Your submission isn't in that hot puff of pain or startling pleasure. They are simply an extension of here."

Once again he rubbed her temple. "Here." He moved her hand so it rested over her pounding heart. "Here."

Her heart seemed to stutter when his mouth brushed over hers. He turned her so she wasn't contorting against him. Doyle Kole was kissing her. That realization made her brain scatter into millions of pieces as his lips parted. She gripped the front of his shirt. He smelled of wood smoke and the ocean and she very much feared every time she smelled either she would think of him. As someone who lived around water and forest, she was doomed.

His fingers fisted in her hair, the tiny pulls making her gasp. She felt his lips curl in a grin before his mouth slanted over hers and the kiss was so beyond what she had dreamed of. It was strength and control, dominating, as he took her lips. His tongue didn't so much as dip into her mouth as it utterly conquered. The slight sweetness that clung to him almost seemed wrong. He should taste dark and smoky. A familiar taste, but she didn't have time to recall because his tongue moved over hers. Utter possession.

Kate rose up on her toes, eager and willing, taking every bold, invading plunge.

Yes and *please* and *Sir.*

Teeth nipped at her and the sting made her blood hum. Hands gripped under her arms and he dragged her up his body. Automatically Kate wrapped her legs around him. A hand slapped onto her ass; the sharp contact hurt even through her jeans. He swallowed the startled sound she made, his hand caressing under her shirt before he pinched the skin at the small of her back.

His laugh was wicked as he turned and carried her into the bedroom. He threw her onto the bed. Threw her. Before her body had time to soak into the softness of the covering, he grabbed her ankles and yanked her toward him. He gazed down at her as his thumb rested against her mouth, the underside of his ring pressing. She felt the band against her lips as he caressed her. "Now it carries your kiss. Want to see what's in my bag?"

She nodded and he dragged the bag over. Whatever

was in it clanked and clinked. Nerves began to prick at her as he zipped it open, the edges gaping. At his nod, she reached in and pulled out the first thing her fingers encountered. A simple flogger. Smooth leather strips that disappeared into the braided grip. She petted it and loved the silky texture on one side of the strip and the rough untreated side of the other.

She watched as his fingers curled around the grip while he lifted her arm.

"The beauty of this is that it can tease." Breathing became a little difficult as he feathered the collection of strips over her arm. "It's sensual. Even to watch it dance on the skin, but like everything in that bag, it can turn on you."

She cried out when he snapped his wrist down. The sting and hot burn hit her skin, then sank deeper. Even as she tried to comprehend the pain, he was painting it lightly over the red spot.

"Now imagine it over every naked inch of you. Wondering, waiting, trying to anticipate when it will hurt, where it will hurt." There was a bark of the leather on denim as it struck her thigh and her vision blurred. It hurt. Holy hell, it hurt even as he once more caressed it up and down her arm. Fingers pressed against her chest and he pushed her to her back. Her eyes closed as he swished it lightly over her breasts and down her stomach. She arched and was rewarded with his hand slipping between her legs. The tease of the flogger and the erotic stroking of his fingers were almost too much. She gasped as he brushed the ends over her face.

His hand gripped her hip and he eased her onto her side.

"The good old fashioned strap." She screamed as he snapped something from hell down on her ass. Hot. Burning. Ow. "It's subtle, isn't it?"

Ow. She rubbed her ass and glared at him. He smirked as he tossed the thick strip of leather to the foot of the bed. "Handcuffs. Padded cuffs." He tossed them onto the bed beside her and she reached for the padded ones, exploring them. "Spreader bar."

He eased off her shoes and socks. Kate rose up on her elbows and watched as he strapped one ankle in, then the other. Hands caught under her knees and he jerked, dragging her toward him as her legs bent. When he held out his right hand, she gave him the cuffs. She was breathing fast as he wrapped each wrist and hooked them to her ankles.

"Take it in, girl," he said, stroking over her legs. "Slowly in."

She slowed her breathing down, matching the glide of his hands up and down her thighs.

"Condoms." There was the rustle of the box opening and the wrapper slid over her stomach as he tucked it behind the fly of her jeans. "Lube." He tossed it above her head. "Old reliable." He waggled a butt plug, setting it down on the bed. "The newest edition courtesy of J, who is diabolical." He held up two bars. "Haven't used it yet." He parted them and held them to his chest. "Not tonight, but one day I'm going to imprison your nipples in this and play." It clanked as he put it back in the bag. "My favorite. The crop. But not yet. Let's save that." He reached for the flogger, and if she could have, she'd have squeezed her thighs together.

He bared her stomach and danced it lightly over her

skin, drawing lazy circles. She arched, her body chasing the sensual touches over her breasts, down her arms. There was a soft growl and he eased her onto her stomach. He freed her hands and moved her so her feet rested on the floor.

He stripped her shirt off and snapped open her bra before he brushed the leather over her skin. Gasping, she fisted her hands, clutching the duvet. The bed muffled her cry when he began to strike a little harder. An angle down her back one side, then the other, like he was making Xs over her skin.

A hard, painful slash over her ass and she arched at the fire because not even the denim had been able to muffle that.

"You good?"

She nodded and fingers tangled in her hair, jerking her head back and pulling her until his face was there. Right. Words. "Yes."

He rolled her over and she bowed as the cool sheet hit hot skin that stung even though he hadn't hit hard. She lifted her hips when she felt the zipper go and he drew down her jeans, stripping her naked after removing the spreader bar. The feel of him fully clothed against her bare skin made her gasp. Two fingers slid into her and his mouth swallowed her cry.

So much Doyle. His tongue matched the erotic movement of his fingers. Her back felt as if she had been out in the sun just five minutes too long while her ass burned and throbbed in time to his stroking fingers. The taste of him, that outdoorsy smell of him, the weight of him.

"Let go, my girl. All that I told you to hold in, let go."

"Doyle." She hooked her legs over his, loving the rasp of denim over skin that felt new. Against the inside of her thigh she could feel the hard press of his cock and she remembered how it felt inside her. A hundred times better than his fingers because he had been everywhere inside, not an inch of her untouched, unclaimed by him. She cried out, arching into him, her hips jerking as he slid a third finger into her. She loved the way the burn on her ass rubbed over the sheet.

"Let go, Katey. Now."

Her body shuddered as the most intense orgasm of her life moved through her. His hand spread over the small of her back, holding her against him as she shuddered over the fingers thrusting and caressing inside her. So much Doyle.

"You remember how you told me about that moment? That one that makes you come in the darkness of your bedroom?"

She nodded.

"This is that moment. Where the scene quietly ends. The pain is nothing but a memory on the skin, the mind-fuck is over." She shuddered as his fingers slid from her. "The moment of surrender. When you surrendered all to my hands. Trust with your pain, trust with your pleasure. The moment that's yours. What's the moment, Katey? Tell me."

"When she's his."

"When you're mine." He thrust into her.

She cried out his name, because everywhere. He was everywhere.

"Look at me, Katey."

She opened her eyes and focused on the black gaze

watching her as he thrust inside her. Every stroke made her gasp and rise into him. He grabbed the back of his shirt and dragged it off, baring all the ink up his arms, the ripple of the muscles as he moved to an erotic rhythm she matched. *When you're mine.*

"Doyle," she mouthed and her eyes fluttered closed.

"Come for me, Katey. Come for me."

She shuddered as she grabbed the sheets and his fingers spread over her wrists. The contact made her splinter apart. The orgasm rocked through her as he drove deep into her. So much Doyle. She felt the hard shudder that moved through him as he buried himself in her one last time.

She had been wrong.

This was the most intense orgasm of her life. A hand caressed over her cheek, tilted her head and he kissed her. The sweetest kiss of her life and that was what finally broke her.

When you're mine.

Kate - 2002

He was home! The sound of laughter and music drew her down the stairs. The sweet acrid smell of pot mingled with the voices and she sat down. At this angle she could see Jace on the couch. Some movie was on the television but there was no sound. It was all about the music. Resting her elbows on her knees, she cupped her chin in her hands and watched Jace. He was back.

He had gone to Las Vegas with Shaelynn, according to Mrs. Dawson. Not to get married, as Jace's girlfriend had assumed, but simply to party for a week. The housekeeper had been horrified to realize she had forgotten Kate and had stayed at the house, apologizing profusely and making Kate all kinds of cookies and cakes. It had been surprisingly hard to forgive the older woman. What had made Mrs. Dawson finally remember her? Her uniform.

Something had cracked away inside her that day. Blossoming hope that everything would be okay was gone. Long gone. No amount of chocolate chip cookies would make her believe again.

The rest of the band was here. She recognized them from the case of the CD she had bought with some of the money Jace gave her. With the discman she had also bought with the money, she'd lie under her bed and listen to him sing while she carefully took the booklets part to tape his pictures up beneath her bed. She had quite the collage going. She recognized Carl Hughes, who played the guitar. He was at the bar, pouring a drink, while Anderson Reeve, who played bass, could be heard but not seen. She didn't quite know the difference between a bass and guitar, only that they were different. There was another guitar player, Maximillian Jones, and Doyle Kole who was the drummer, but she didn't see them.

Not that she really cared about them.

Jace was home. He had come back.

He laughed, disappearing behind the sofa. When he came up he shook his head and pinched his nose. The sight made her stomach twist. Once she had found a needle in his bedroom and she had been terrified she'd find him dead somewhere like Mom.

Deep laughter came from behind her and panic hit. *Hide, hide, hide.* Before she could, a large body came half running down the stairs. His eyes went wide as he realized he was in a collision course with her. She scrambled off the step and into the basement that smelled like the trailer.

Funny, that didn't change. She looked down, wondering where the stained, cracked linoleum was but it was just soft white carpet.

"Shit. Nearly trampled her." The guy pressed a hand over his chest. "Gotta remember we have little people around."

A snort made her look and stare. She wanted to scramble back and find a hiding place. She wanted the safety of under her bed. Because he was big. The biggest man she had ever seen. He had no hair on the sides of his head and his black hair shot up in sharp, angry spikes. She knew mean eyes like his. It meant fists. Mom had eyes like that. They narrowed and he crouched down, bracing a hand on the floor so they were eye level.

"Who are you?" His voice was so low it added to that urge to hide. The smells, the noise, those mean eyes. She wanted to go home. She wanted Mom.

His eyes were just mean looking. They were black with red in the white. She knew what that meant too. Eyes just like Mom. Mom had hated it when Kate hadn't answered her questions and since he looked like he could crush her with one hit, she decided to answer.

"Kate Jace Jennings," she whispered, her throat too dry from fear for her to speak any louder. Something ugly came into his eyes and she hunched a bit, waiting.

She twisted one of the knots holding her ribbon from side to side.

"Fuck, you look just like him. Don't you, Katey Jay?"

He sounded like that was a bad thing so she kept still. A grunt came from him. When someone called, "D" he turned around and walked away.

Kate tried to make herself as small as possible as she watched Cyanide. Her gaze locked on Jace, hungry for the sight of him even as she wished he had been the one to call her Katey Jay.

Chapter 8

THERE WAS SOMETHING to be said about waking up to a warm, naked body in his bed. Rising up on one arm, he caressed the slightly flushed skin on Kate's back. He hadn't hit hard enough to leave a mark, but there was definite evidence he had been there. *Nice.* His stomach let out a not so subtle rumble and he slid out of the bed.

His internal clock was still syncing up with the real world. Naked, he walked into the kitchen, leaving the lights off. All remnants of the party on Friday were gone. They had the best cleaning crew. The pantry was once more stocked with non-perishables while the fridge was filled with everything from milk to soda to wine. He grabbed the milk and a box of Cheerios. Once his snack was ready, he leaned against the island and looked out the wall of windows.

"How can you be naked with so many windows?"

He held the spoon in his mouth as he studied Kate wearing one of his shirts. Her hair was messed up from his grabby hands and her lips were a little redder than usual, swollen from his kisses. Sex-rumpled Kate was a thing of beauty. From the fruit bowl she picked up an apple, washing it off in the sink.

"First, they're reflective and second, it's liberating. If someone gets a peek, well, look at all this." A soft chuckle escaped from her when he waved his hand over his body. He picked her up, set her on the island and leaned between her legs. A foot rubbed his hip while the crisp sound of her taking a bite of her apple filled the growing silence. Juice squirted onto his shoulder and fingers wiped the specks away. "I should make you wander around here naked."

Her fingers stilled against his skin and his cock went heavy at the idea of watching a naked Kate. Something to ponder when she wasn't expecting it.

"This place doesn't even look the same."

He nodded as he braced his hands on either side of her thighs. Everything sparkled. The cleaning team who came in the night after the party earning the fat pay check they received. "You mentioned support groups," he said and he glanced over when she rested her cheek on his shoulder, gazing out the windows. "What made you go?"

She was quiet and he waited as his thumb caressed her knee. "I heard about Edge but knew…it's hard fearing something you want. That bad sex I told you about? He was an online hook-up through a kink site."

"What is it with you and the douche doms?"

He caught her hand and flattened it on his stomach, his thumb brushing over the bracelet.

"You're not a douche."

"I'm an asshole. I'm the next level. Was it like the dom at Edge?" He laid his palm against hers and the size difference was beyond obvious.

"No. He actually talked about stuff. Asked me some things. But it wasn't good. I couldn't get there. You know?"

She broke his heart. "You don't get there. There's not a direct route like a bus. You didn't stop the scene." Neither had the dom. He hated irresponsibility when it came to topping.

"No. I wanted it so bad, Doyle." Her voice cracked and he turned. He caught her head and she lowered it to his shoulder. "I'm not good at this. Even when it's a good dom, I mess up."

"You have some messed up idea about what being a sub means, Katey." Doyle scooped her off the island and carried her into the enclosed living room. Sure there were the windows she complained about, but there were walls to give it an intimate feel. He turned on the fireplace and sat on one of the leather couches. Not the most comfortable sensation against his naked ass but he sucked it up. She straddled his lap, studying the tattoos on his arm as a way of avoiding him. She traced one on his biceps. A rotting apple that bled into a skull. Her thumb swept over the band's name in a banner beneath it.

It wasn't the band's typeface or logo. Just a reflection of what his band was. Toxic. Poison. They had picked the name Cyanide wisely, though they had picked it because it sounded bad ass.

"Why do you think you're not good at this?"

"Because I always do something wrong. If it's not good and I'm the common denominator, then I'm doing something wrong."

Hm. With the edge of her fingernail she traced out the letters and the light scratching was making his cock ache. How she didn't seem to notice the shirt was snagged over his hard on was mind boggling, but she wasn't in a good head space to notice much.

"I can't snap my fingers and get you there. This isn't a hypnotist show on a stage. I told you earlier, it starts in the head." He caressed her calves and she nodded in response, though he felt like she didn't believe him. "It starts here." He laid his hand between her breasts. "The foundation of all BDSM play, no matter your kink, is trust, Katey. You're trusting me with your body. You're trusting me to hurt you, but in a way that won't leave a scar on your body and here." His fingers pressed against her chest. "You're trusting me to not treat you like a puppet when I demand something, whether it's for you to hold in an orgasm or kneel at my feet." She was watching him now, her eyes hidden beneath the shield of her lashes but she was paying attention. "You don't obey because you're weak and have no mind of your own. You obey because it makes me feel good and it makes you feel good. Sometimes something goes south. Sometimes the worries here," he feathered his thumb over her forehead, "are bigger than the both of us. Maybe it's because it was your very first time or you have trust issues. Your mother was negligent, your father let you down continuously; you feel small and lost and there's this horrific thing crowding up on you, taking over. Swallowing you down and down because you were hurt in the most vulnerable way. So yeah, that first time isn't going to go good. But it's not because you're doing something wrong. It's because he's not looking into your pretty green eyes and seeing that you are lost in the weeds."

A tear slid down her cheek and he wiped it away. "Your eyes, Katey Jay, hold no secrets. He should've seen.

It's his job to pay attention to the details. I'm going to see if my sub isn't doing well. It's in her eyes. It's in the way her body tenses instead of flows with a touch or a word. It's her voice if she's struggling. If, for whatever reason my sub isn't going to safe word, I'm going to stop it. We're going to slow down until it works and if it doesn't, it doesn't."

"I threw up all over your balcony."

"Someone threw up in my hot tub, Kate. People were puking in plants and in someone's purse. One of the most stunning things I have ever seen in my life was you on that very balcony. You so lost in what you wanted from me was beyond erotic. Watching you not just slide into subspace, but sink into it, is amazing. It makes me want to put you there all the time. It makes me want to carry you over my shoulder into Edge to give you that need. Nothing went south tonight. We're just having a small drop."

He tumbled her to the couch and she stared at him; the need in her gaze could put him to his knees. The need to believe him. "I want you to tell me that first pivotal moment where the light bulb went on and you went 'Oh.'"

"Will you tell me yours first?"

He stretched out, his back to the room. "It was during the video shoot of Other Side. Not our best song, but that's what happens when I'd rather get drunk and leave the writing to Carl, Anderson and Jace."

"You're so modest, Doyle."

He grinned. "I know. I need to work on that." He brushed her hair off her face. "It was doing mediocre on the charts and there was a lot of pressure for us to not suck as it was the second album. So when they decided that we needed a video, the director pitched an edgy idea. I was drinking when I watched them tie this girl up to a St. Andrew's Cross and it hit all my buttons. There I am standing there and my cock is hard because it was the most erotic thing I had seen. When they said one of us needed to be the dom I was all over that role. It was one of the few times I came alive. They brought someone in to show me what to do because hurting one of the actresses would've sucked, but it wasn't like I could tap the air. I was rocking massive wood that entire video shoot and I may or may not have fucked some of the girls between takes because… Jesus. It was amazing." The video had been banned pretty much everywhere. It had been the early nineties; shit like that didn't fly. Thanks to online videos and that book, the video's viewings had skyrocketed a couple of years ago. The song still sucked, but the video was hot.

The consultant had been an actual dom and had taken Doyle under his wing as kind of his mentor. The friendship had become pretty important to him and when James had been killed, Doyle had spiraled out of control. It had, in fact, been one of the early coffin nails in his marriage.

"I watch that video," Kate confessed. His attention snapped to her face and the blush on her cheeks.

"Is it in your spank box, Miss Jennings?" The blush spread further and she gave a small nod.

"I turn off the sound and," she shrugged one shoulder, "you know."

He slid his hand between her legs. "Like this?" She was already slippery and her mouth parted on a tiny gasp.

"Use your words, Katey."

"Yes, Sir," she whispered.

"Show me what you do when the sound is off and you watch me beat three girls. Do you pretend you're one?"

"I imagine I'm the only," she admitted. Her fingers covered his, shifting him so his fingertip grazed her clit. Her hips rocked up and a sexy, soft sound came from her. She drew circles around that tender bud, using him to get herself off, lost in the fantasy. "There's that one shot of you when you're standing with your hand braced on the cross. The camera pans over your face and you mouth the word come to her."

"Do you come when I tell you too?"

"Every time, Sir. Every time."

Doyle exhaled slowly and lowered his head so his lips brushed her ear. "Come," he whispered. She cried out, her body straining up as she came. "Every time you call me Sir, my cock throbs to be inside you, aches to lay claim to you. It makes me want to take you over and take you under." He slid two fingers into her and felt her clutch his wrist. "It slips off your tongue and I want to taste it, own it. You say it as easily as you say my name. Easier. You'll drop it into a text and I want you there because I get fucking hard as hell. Each time, every time, I want to fuck you until it whispers from your soul. I want you on your knees as I fuck that word along your tongue. Come." Her orgasm was beautiful.

He opened the side table drawer and withdrew a condom, slipping it on. He moved between her legs and rubbed his thumb over her mouth. Her lips parted and the tip of her tongue touched his skin, the ring she gave him, and he sank into her, her cry sinking into him. "Jesus, look at you." He thrust into her, her pussy snug from her orgasms, her body meeting his as she wrapped her legs around him, her fingers digging into his back. He wanted to give her every fantasy in her head. He wanted to not fuck up and satisfy that need that glowed in her eyes.

He wanted to make sure she never doubted herself in this because she was so beautiful when she submitted, so deep in subspace he could taste it on her skin. "Christ, Kate." He kissed her, his tongue sliding over hers and there was that honeyed taste. He wished he had kissed her before he had topped her so he knew if this is was what her submission tasted like or if it was pure Kate. The leather creaked beneath their bodies while the gas flames flickered.

Not even Claire had felt this good. Right. Fuck. How the hell…

He wanted to come in her. Strip off the condom and come in her so she was marked. Every hidden inch of her coated in his cum. So she felt him on her thighs and knew that he had been there, that his cum made her his.

God, he wanted to come in her. Now. "Come," he demanded against her lips and sweet little subbie that she was, she did. He drank down her cry while fucking hard into her as she came until he had to obey too. Come.

They stilled, breaths mingling. This girl who wore the face of the man he hated. She was in his skin, in his blood. Oz had been right. The minute he had caught a whiff that Kate was a submissive, he had watched. Wanted. Craved. Waited. Like that first time during the video shoot when he had held that crop. Like all the pieces of him finally made sense.

Fuck but he had missed being someone's dom.

Kate traced the names that were entwined in a heart on Doyle's chest: Claire, Willow, Danielle. It was a tattoo so at odds with the others. He watched her through lowered lids, his fingers tracing up and down her spine. The t-shirt had disappeared at some point. His other arm was bent behind his head.

Her gaze shifted to an upside-down creepy sun. She traced the jagged rays and moved to the zombie trying to crawl through his skin as if that sun was summoning it. No flowers, no tribal, no normal looking animals. She knew somewhere on his left arm there was a drum stick that was staked through a skull, there was an executioner with a bloody axe, because in the tattoo magazines they always focused on a couple. If they were doing a body shot, his hand would rest on his chest, like he was protecting those three names. The realization made her chest feel tight.

They were so lucky.

Sometimes she wondered if Jace even knew her name.

"How old were you, Katey?"

She continued to explore the dark images forever on his arm. She tried to answer but had to clear her throat to continue. "Twelve." Her voice sounded scratchy. Broken.

He went still beneath her. "No." It was stark and blunt and sliced into her chest like heated metal.

"Twelve," she repeated on a whisper. Twelve. She went to move, but Doyle flattened his hand on her, keeping her still. "I can't like this. Please." She slid down to the other end of the couch and he sat up, easing his leg from behind her. He rested his elbow on his bent leg, his inked fingers forming a loose fist at his mouth. Needing contact more than she thought she would, she leaned against his leg, the dark hair soft against her skin, while she rested her head against one of his dark and twisty tattoos.

With his other hand, he cupped her cheek, his thumb catching every tear that began to escape. For the first time in a long time, she felt safe. His hand made her think of those pictures where he was protecting the heart on his chest. Made her think he was protecting her too. *Aways wanting.*

Kate - 2002

She had never had a Christmas tree before. Sitting on the couch, watching the large fir tree being decorated, Kate decided it was the most beautiful thing she had ever seen. This morning she had woken to find the house overrun by a woman with a clipboard and clear plastic bins filled with all kinds of decorations. There was something very efficient about her as she directed an army of people on where to put things. Shaelynn sashayed about telling people what she wanted, but the clipboard woman ignored her.

There was going to be a photo shoot because apparently there had been some bad publicity with the band trashing a club and walking off in the middle of a set. The band's manager, Charles Haversley, had decided they needed good publicity and what was better than a girl's first Christmas? Ever. So now the house was under holiday siege for the photo shoot and interview, even though

Christmas wasn't for a while.

Kate didn't care.

This was unlike anything she had ever seen. Shaelynn had said they needed a black Christmas tree with white and silver decorations so it fit with the decor of the house. Everyone, even Jace, had looked at her like she was crazy. Black fake Christmas trees didn't say "we're celebrating Kate's first Christmas. Ever!"

A catering service was going to provide them with a turkey dinner because apparently that's what families did at Christmas. The entire band and their families were coming later because this was all about salvaging their reputation.

Kate didn't care.

She knew none of this was real, but that didn't stop the warm glow from growing in her chest. The tree was becoming something beautiful, magical. Lights blinked and glowed. Some were flickering white ones and others were clearly for Halloween because they were little white skulls, because they were, to quote Jace, bad ass. The tree was rock and roll. Jace had said the only way he was going to do this was if they didn't make some cotton candy, pussy decorations.

She wasn't entirely sure what that meant, but this was not a tree she'd see in the mall.

The hair stylist arrived and not just for Shaelynn. According to her, Kate also had to be treated so she didn't look like a homeless waif who was living off their kindness.

So she found herself getting her hair washed and blowed dried.

"That one is a right a bitch," the guy with the hair

dryer and a round brush said as he made Kate's hair look soft and shiny.

"You'd think she was screwing someone important instead of a fading rock star. What do you think of this one?"

"Too frou-frou."

Kate watched as dresses were held up and discarded. All of them were so pretty so to see them flung onto her bed as if they weren't important, made something tighten in her chest. She twisted a knot in her ribbon, worrying it back and forth as she watched as another dress was lifted then flung aside when it was nixed. She had no idea where the clothes had come from.

"This is not a frou-frou face." The hairdresser cupped her chin and tilted her head up, studying her. She wished she remembered his name. He was nice and that he didn't like Shaelynn made him even better. He smelled of cologne and had vibrant blue streaks in his black hair, plus he wore make-up. Who did that?

"No, it's not." The clothes flinger tapped a finger against his mouth. "It's a sweet face. Far too sweet for this house. Hm. Angelic. Let me see…"

"Old eyes," her stylist said as he returned to making her hair glossy and straight. "Let's not emphasize that. This is about joy, not the heartache in those eyes. That won't help Jace Jennings out if the world saw the sadness in his daughter's eyes."

She blinked at the word daughter. She looked down her ribbon, mentally mapping the way the ribbon made the knots. Being called Jace's daughter by someone made her body tingle while her heart felt like it was trying to explode from her chest.

"Oh, that's it. That's the one."

She looked at the dress in the mirror, turning in the chair to stare. It was a soft silver color and was the prettiest thing she had ever seen. She wanted to stroke her hand over the fabric. Thin strips of fabric reminded her of ribbons. Along the top and the straps were shiny silver sequins.

"The color isn't what they wanted, but if we put her in a bold color with a heavy fabric she'll be overwhelmed. Go tell Jace's stylist we changed the color. Must have them coordinated."

"The bitch with the bump?"

"She's a big girl."

Reaching out, Kate brushed her fingers over the fragile strips. "Wow," she whispered. They dressed her, and sent her off. Shaelynn was in a body-hugging red dress that showed the world she was going to have Jace's baby. Her hair looked like gold had been poured over her. Jace looked bored as he stood there in black pants and a pale grey shirt.

"Okay, try to look like you give a damn," Charles said as he came over to study her. "Not the look I was wanting, but there is something to you. Okay, happy faces, Jace, and let's save your ass."

She watched as Jace popped a pill and chased it with scotch. He handed his glass to his assistant and flashed a smile at her.

Just like the house, she was going to pretend. She was going to pretend this was real because she wanted it to be like this. Not just Christmas, but every day. If she believed in Santa, she'd ask for this moment to last forever and to be real. So, she pretended it was because she was had little hope in Christmas really being like this. She wanted this magic. She wanted Jace to smile at her, to see her.

Always wanting.

Chapter 9

FOR THE FIRST time in a long time, Kate dreamed of him. He slipped through the cobwebs of her dreams. He slithered like a snake and hunted like a shark. The predator to her prey and her brain told her that this wasn't real but he was there. "Hello, pretty little No One."

With a gasp, she sat up and was momentarily confused. Not her room. Once that registered, she kicked off the sheets and tumbled out of Doyle's bed, sprinting for the bathroom. The tile was icy beneath her feet and hurt when her knees crashed down. At least she wasn't throwing up on his deck. Stupid thought as she heaved over the toilet. Light exploded, making her head hurt because this much light was too much. A much larger hand than hers gathered up her hair but she didn't want him touching her. Not now. Not with *him* there. "Don't." She pushed against Doyle's stomach, moaned, then let the acid out, let *him* out.

Doyle crouched down beside her and she just wanted him away. "Go. Away." She shoved him as she screamed and he caught her hands.

"Okay." He squeezed her fingers and left her as she felt her throat squeeze and twist. Her stomach rebelled.

The tears came as the bathroom was plunged into darkness. From the other side of the narrow tiled wall, she heard the roar of water as he filled the tub. More tears came because he hadn't left her. Her hand was shaking when she flushed the toilet and she leaned against the wall, too beaten down to get up. That was when Doyle appeared.

"Rinse, girl." He held a glass out to her and she took a mouthful of minty water, swished, and spat it into the toilet. Another rinse and he tucked a toothbrush in her hand with a brisk, "Brush, girl."

She brushed, rinsed the last of the acidic taste away and watched, too limp to move, as he took the glass and toothbrush from her. He was back, scooping her up like she weighed nothing. The tub was filling with water and bubbles and tears escaped because no one had ever prepped a bubble bath for her. He stepped in and sank down, lowering her into warm water. Doyle stretched out at the other end, watching her. Always watching.

You know your tub is big when Doyle Kole could sit in it with room to spare.

When the water reached her breasts and the bubbles were a fluffy, cool cloud at her shoulders, he turned off the faucet. Staring at him was too much. She turned, rising onto her knees so she could look out the window, see his reflection in the glass. With her breasts flattened against the wall of the tub, Kate pillowed her head on her folded arms and gazed out at the night.

A bare foot slid up and down her back, contact so she would know she wasn't alone. That was, however, the extent of their communication.

She didn't know how long she ignored him, though

it was hard to ignore Doyle. The bubbles popped and he added more hot water, but he didn't say anything. He was just there.

It was enough.

"I used to watch you do that with Claire. She'd be kneeling on the floor, and you'd rub your foot over her back. It took a while to figure out why she was always kneeling. She was your sub."

"Yes. The floor was her choice though. Try explaining why your eight month pregnant wife prefers kneeling. It was a little easier when Willy was born because there was a visible reason of why Claire was down there. She still kneels; just for someone else now."

Kate cupped some water in her hand, spilling along the smooth surface of the tub, watching it trickle into the bath water. She peeked at the window and saw Doyle sat with one arm bent, his head resting on his fist as he watched her. Watched over her.

"I used to wonder if you married her because she was pregnant but that would've been a pretty epic pregnancy. I mean, that's why everyone else got married."

"I married Claire because I loved her. Antiquated idea, I know."

"What happened?" She shifted sideways so she could see him. He ran his foot up her side to her arm and back to her hip. "Can I ask that?"

Dark eyes watched her. "You can ask me anything you want, Katey. I got clean. When we learned she was pregnant with Willy, she told me to shape up or ship out. It was a moment of clarity. I loved her. I didn't want to lose my wife. I didn't want to lose my sub. I didn't want to lose my daughter. I didn't want to lose myself. It was happening. I could see it, reflected in Andy. My drugs were getting harder and he gave me some bad shit. I wound up in the hospital. There was my pregnant wife, crying because she was so scared I was going to die on her, but if I did that would be okay because she was tough enough to raise the baby on her own. Nothing like learning you're superfluous."

He let out some of the cold water and refilled the tub with hot, watching the flow. "So I checked myself into rehab. There are few people I want to emulate. Anderson Reeves and Jace Jennings are on that short list. Detoxing is hell. Don't go through that. Your body turns inside out and you can feel your soul being strangled in all the shit that's oozing out of you. We were good for a while. I was a better version of me but I was still me." He flicked off the water and returned to his position.

"I was still an asshole, still full of anger and hate, but only now I had nothing to hide behind. When Willy was born, there was this perfect human being *I* was responsible for creating. Jesus, Katey. She was beautiful. Is beautiful. Then came Dani and it was like my life was getting better and better. Sober I was way better as a dom, which works when you're a kinky couple. Problem is when you find your wife fucking someone else you realize you were shitting yourself, that the dream was fragmented all along. We fought. About stupid shit. I was never around. Why did she have to deal with potty training? The baby was sick but what good was I if I was in Germany? Who was I fucking? It just swelled until the walls collapsed and it was over."

"She slept with Jace. Didn't she?"

His gaze locked on hers and he nodded once. "On

purpose. Knowing they'd get caught. Knowing I hate that cocksucker. Because someone needed to pull the trigger and Claire felt that was the only way."

She rested her cheek on her knee and looked out the window. Jace Jennings was a horrible human being. "Am I here out of some form of revenge? He slept with your wife so you're fucking his daughter?"

"No."

He didn't say anything further. The water rippled against her as he moved. An arm hooked around her waist and he drew her between his legs.

"Nobody is in this but you and I, Kate."

She rested against him and traced one of the tattoos on his forearm. "Why are these so dark and twisty?"

"Aside from Andy, we all came from shit. When you come from the shadow places, it leaves an impact. These all represent what I saw when I looked in the mirror."

"And now?"

He pressed his lips against her shoulder. "They still resonate."

That made her sad. He turned his arm so she could trace the words *Do not go gentle* that met a sinister moon. On his other inner arm was more of the Dylan Thomas poem *Rage against the dying* that met a candle snuffed out. Out of all his tattoos, the poem quotes were the ones that got her the most. "What is this? You said this, but what is it?"

"I don't know, but we'll figure it out. Tell me about this." His hand dipped beneath the water and his fingers circled her own tattoo.

"I wanted to be *able* to look in the mirror. To not fear. To remind myself sex isn't about hate and evil."

His sigh rubbed against her back. "Claire was right. You *are* strong. I want to push you, to get it all out but I'm won't."

"Why?"

"Because I want to know for me. I want to know who so I can hurt him. I want to make him bleed. I want him to know fear so that when he hears a Cyanide song or sees me, I'm a trigger for his fear. I want to put him in the ground."

"It won't change anything, Doyle."

"Don't care."

She touched the evil moon, tracing its cynical smirk. A part of her wanted him to push, to make her tell him everything. A larger part wanted it to not factor at all. For the most part it didn't. He didn't haunt her thoughts or waking hours. "I made a promise to myself a few years ago."

"Tell me."

"That only two people would ever control me, would ever have power over me. Not the ghosts of my past, not the demons who stalked them. Me and—"

She cried out, arching as he suddenly pushed two fingers hard into her. "Me," he growled in her ear. Oh. Oh, God. The cooling water lapped against her skin as he moved within her, his touch conquering and erasing her thoughts while wiping away the nightmare. Against the small of her back she felt the hot press of his cock, his other hand sliding between her legs where he rubbed and pressed against her clit.

Her hands gripped the hard swells of his biceps, surging with every push. *My dom,* she finished her head, unable to voice the words because that meant thinking.

Her feet skated along the tub, trying to find a purchase until his legs trapped them.

She felt his teeth close over the tendon at her neck, scraping just hard enough so she could feel each tooth. Her brain emptied at all he did.

"Ready?"

"Yes, Sir." Her neck arched as he bit the curve at her collarbone.

"Take it in." He slowly bit his way along to her shoulder, every time just a little bit harder. That pain coupled by what he was doing between her legs made her feel like she was sinking into the water, being swallowed up. Reaching up to cup the back of his head to give him more of her arm, she could only gasp at it all. Her other hand reached down to grab his thigh.

"God, you're so fucking wet, so already there, aren't you, girl? I can tell by the way you gasp, draw in your breath, the way your cunt welcomes me inside. Already there," he murmured as he sucked on a spot where he had bitten. "I want to beat you and fuck you."

The words made her gasp audibly, arching from him in an attempt to get closer.

"You have no idea how badly I wanted to tie you to that railing in the club, bend you over so I could turn your little ass red, sinking my cock so far in you it would take hours to get out."

"Oh. Oh, God."

"See what you miss out on when you run?"

She was going to come. She felt it brewing just beyond where his fingers touched and tormented. "Doyle!"

"I like Sir," he whispered. "Hold it in." His fingers slid from her and she whimpered at the sensation. The solid presence of him vanished from behind her but the hand on her shoulder kept her upright. Her body was humming from the heady combination of pleasure and pain, of the overwhelming presence that was Doyle. There was a roaring in her head and she swore she could feel the blood in her veins as it traveled to all the sensitive spots from his bites to her clit. He lifted her out of the tub, the gurgle of draining water letting her know what the roar was.

"Hands like this. Don't move." He braced her forearms against the cool glass, her palms flat, and she stared blankly at the glitter beyond her. Lights. Window. Doyle. She watched his reflection as he used his foot to spread her legs. He grabbed a towel from under the sink and she watched him leave her there, canted forward and Vancouver on the other side of the glass.

Water slid down her body, slipping over skin that felt hypersensitive from the orgasm that hovered just out of reach, denied by him. Between the cool window and the heat still clinging to her from Doyle, it was all about contrast. The dry air on her wet skin, the unquenched ache in her pussy, the pleasant hurt from his teeth.

The soft slap of bare feet, but she didn't look. Looking meant moving.

"Nice. You're responsible for this." He lifted her left hand and pressed a foil packet in place then laid her hand back down. At the feel of the condom, her knees went watery. A condom meant sex and that made things want. His hands at her ankles made her stare at the ghostly reflection as he set the spreader bar in place.

"Oh, God," she whispered.

"If you drop the condom," Doyle warned in an evil

voice, "I won't fuck you. Do you want me to fuck you, Katey Jay?"

"Yes, Sir."

"Don't drop it."

She licked her lips and he pressed something firm against her back. Against the back of her legs she felt the rough fibers of the towel though it did nothing to hide the swell of his cock that he tucked in the crease of her ass. Oh. *God.*

"I like a wet Katey Jay in my bathroom, her nipples hard from a combination of arousal and cool air. It makes me want to put things on them. Deep breath, girl." A sharp pressure made her cry out, her ass push back into him and a trickle of cream to spill from the sudden spasm of her sex. He eased the clamp a smidge until it was a low, steady ache and caressed her stomach. "Another." Now she knew what was coming. Her fingers curled before she remembered the condom and she flattened her hands. He chuckled—diabolical asshole—as he adjusted the other clamp. A heavy silver chain swung back and forth as she struggled for her breath. He caressed a hand over her hair and a soft, "take it in," was repeated against her ear until she sank into the pain. "There we go. Don't forget the condom."

"No, Sir."

The press of Doyle's body disappeared and she tried to focus on his reflection, she really did, but things were humming behind her eyes, her body not quite there anymore. Knuckles caressed over her buttocks and there was a sharp, hard smack. She cried out as the pain exploded beneath the skin and sank deep. The second bark of her skin taking another strike made her shudder. The sound, the feel, the gentle touch over her ass.

"You never did tell me when your submission light flashed green for go. We'll have to get to that."

A third blow, this time lower on her thighs, made her cry out, made her struggle to remember to keep her hand flat because she couldn't drop the condom. She wouldn't. The fourth strike made her forget there was a condom. There was only the bark of the crop, the bite on her breasts, and the bliss of it all.

The towel was rough against sensitive skin as he pressed against her, notching the hard wedge of his cock between her ass once more.

"You still have it?"

She nodded and he had to peel her hand away to free the condom. She felt the towel slide down over every mark, making her hiss while the hot flesh made her push back into him. There was only one remaining untouched spot that craved him.

His hands caught her hips as he rocked against her. She flattened her hand against the window, the dark erotic sensation of him resting between her buttocks, his skin against the marks he had put on her, making her shudder. *His marks on her.*

The realization made her head spin. Fingers curled in her hair and he turned her head. "Look at us, Katey."

It took a moment to remember how to open her eyes. Their reflection in the mirror was beyond erotic, it was sexual and graphic.

"That's how we'll look when I'm deep in your ass. Nice. Not tonight though."

He eased away and she watched him tear open the condom wrapper and flick it to the floor. His decorated fingers rolled the condom on, curled around the length of him and he stroked from tip to base then back again. Sexy. He was sexy. Beautiful. His grin was wicked in the mirror as he shifted and brought his big hand down on her ass.

It was loud in the bathroom and the pain. Holy shit. It shocked her that a hand could make her skin hurt like that, make the muscle beneath twitch and shudder in response.

"My hand, your ass. How many times did I say that to you?"

"Uh three? Four?"

"Let's do five just to be sure."

Oh Lord. Save her from the rhythmic smacks. He didn't spank lightly. It was as if all that power in his arms radiated down to his palm and into her ass.

"Oh baby," he said quietly, "look at you."

Look? That meant opening her eyes, moving. Not that he gave her a chance as he shifted her a smidge and buried his cock deep in her, making her cry out. He sank in until he pressed against her sore bum. She shuddered at the sensation, a tiny whimper of pain that turned into a little sigh of pleasure and only then did he begin to move.

All of it was far better than she had ever imagined. *This*, she thought, *this.*

Kate – December 31, 2002

The party was loud and made her skin crawl: the music, the voices. The sickly sweet pungent smell of marijuana filled the air and alcohol added a bitter smell. From her hiding spot, Kate watched it all. A naked woman with big, bouncy breasts ran by, screaming "Happy new year!" She recognized some famous people. It was hard not to since Shelby loved the gossip magazines. Rock music pumped from the expensive sound system. It wasn't the band's music, or at least she didn't think so.

She saw Carl Hughes making drinks for scantily clad women at the circular bar. His wife had stormed out a while ago. Did he even remember he had a wife now? He tilted a bottle of vodka toward his mouth and the clear fluid spilled freely. Maybe not.

Kate was pretty sure none of them remembered that upstairs three other kids were sleeping. Shelby Reeve and Alexis Hughes were in her room while Travis Hughes got his own room next door. She didn't know what time it was. She knew Trav had finally declared defeat at two and had abandoned them. Her room currently smelled of marijuana since the twins had somehow scored a couple of joints. Kate had passed on trying it. Even ten year old Shelby had taken a drag on it, turned a pale color and ran for the bathroom to throw up. That had made Lex laugh like a hyena.

Trav had smiled lazily, sprawled on her bed while he played his guitar.

Lex had passed out after drinking pretty much an entire bottle of wine. They were only a year older than Kate, but so different.

She didn't know what had taken her from her room that smelled of pot where Lex snored and Shelby curled up beside her.

All she had wanted to do was crawl under her bed as music made the house vibrate. People were everywhere.

Inside, outside. Laughing, screaming, shouting, screwing.

She missed her trailer and her bench.

This world was too loud, too fast, too much.

Kate watched Jace. She always watched him. This was not what she used to dream of as a kid, when she would dream of him rescuing her from the trailer and mom. Where he'd scoop her up and take her away from the filth and drugs.

His world wasn't any different than Mom's. It was just cleaner and richer.

He sat in the curve of the horseshoe-shaped couches. Some girl who barely looked older than the twins was kneeling between his legs, his leather pants open for her. He smoked a cigarette and drank from a glass that never emptied. His face twisted and a few minutes later the girl was done, wiping her mouth and beaming up at him. He winked as he did up his pants and laid her over his lap, her ass pointing at the ceiling. He gave her a hard spank and rose up, reaching into his pocket. A few minutes later he was spilling white powder on her back. Anderson Reeve, the bass player from the band, dropped down beside them while Jace used a black credit card to make lines. Kate watched the girl fumble with Anderson's pants and he leaned over her, drawing a line of coke up his nose.

Jace bent over the woman and took a couple of draws up his own nose. A movie star she knew from movies joined them and when he opened his jeans as he knelt behind the woman, Kate made her escape. No one noticed her. She was invisible. A ghost in this large house that was not the fantasy she had built up.

She knew Jace hated her. Kate knew his girlfriend,

or whatever she was, hated her too. She would get all squinty-eyed as she rubbed her belly where Kate's sibling grew. She didn't know where Shaelynn was. The door to Jace's room had been closed so maybe she had gone to bed. Or she was in the pool. Or wherever. Kate didn't care as she darted for the second curve of stairs that would take her upstairs.

"Well hello, pretty little girl. Who are you?"

She froze, her body recognizing a predator. He was holding a beer and his eyes looked freaky. "No one," she whispered. He stepped toward her, his much larger body swaying to music in his head.

"No one," he repeated as he reached out. Kate flinched as he caught her hair, rubbing it between his fingers. "Have you come to party with us, pretty little No One?"

Her eyes flicked to the stairs, then back at him. She shook her head.

"Have you come to have fun with us, pretty little No One?"

"No," Kate whispered.

"Pity." He caressed her cheek with his finger. "Then you must've come to fuck me."

Her body felt cold and empty, a bitter taste in her mouth that she recognized from the trailer. Fear. Her body knew what to do with it. It recognized fear, just like it recognized a predator. She ran up the stairs. She tripped and her hands slammed onto a step while her shin smacked into one. Using her hands to help her, Kate scrambled up the curving stairs.

Hide. Hide. Hide.

She wanted to crawl under her bed and press her body up against the wall where glossy magazine pictures of Jace were. What if he followed?

And he would.

He wanted to have sex with her even though she was kid. Maybe because she was a kid.

Her hands were damp as they gripped the doorknob, slipping on it. She didn't know if it was her heart or footsteps. The door finally opened and she spilled into the room. She locked it so he couldn't get in because Shelby and Lex were sleeping and they were kids too. They were prettier than her.

Her hands shook so hard as she opened the door to the patio outside. Run, run, run. Hide, hide, hide.

She slammed into a body and screamed. A hand clamped over her mouth and she fought because no, no, no. It was not supposed to be like this. Not here. Not in this world that was supposed to be different, better.

Too bad her dream world had turned into the nightmare of her reality.

Chapter 10

DOYLE WATCHED KATE slowly emerge from sleep. Doyle knew the minute she registered what her body had gone through last night when she wrinkled her nose, winced and groaned. "Everything hurts and it's your fault."

"Just think of it as training for Edge." Doyle ran a finger over her ass and stopped at her hip, tracing one of the marks that was a deep pink. A few hours after he had put her to bed and massaged in Jasmine's special blend of lotion that she called Sub Rub, he had woken them both with some slow lazy sex. He had forgotten how much fun sleeping with someone was. That was something he didn't experience on the road. The groupies were a tissue – use once and discard while the subs he hooked up with at the club were almost as disposable. Kate was a treat. "You know, you still haven't told me when Katey Jay came online. How about you scoot on over here and help me work off this erection."

Her gaze roved and settled on the sheet tented over his cock. She blushed and he'd bet it was a combination of embarrassment and arousal. She pushed up onto her knees and reached out to flatten her hand on his stomach. "Breathe through it."

"Everything." She pouted as she arched her back, stretching. Poor sore sub. He liked the way her breasts rose up. He waited until she scooted close. The sheet slithered over his cock and he ground his teeth at the sensation. Her pupils went wide as he was bared.

Nice.

Bending his leg out of the way, he patted the opened space. When she swiveled on her knees so she was facing him, her gaze just a bit uncertain in trying to figure out what to do next, he moved. He caught the back of her neck. As he uncoiled from the bed, he lowered her head so her ass went up. Opening the drawer, he grabbed what he wanted. Within five seconds, everything was ready. Kate's gaze locked on Old Reliable and now there was full-blown uncertainty in her eyes.

He was sadistic enough to enjoy it.

"You ever used one of these?"

"N-no."

He twisted off the cap on the lube, her eyes tracking every move he made. "That's a pretty ass you have there, Miss Katey." She watched him squirt some of the clear gel onto his fingers before he slid his pinky along that tantalizing crease. "Still wearing some stripes. You take color well. Oh the fun we can have with that."

"We? What's this 'we' business?"

He waggled fingers at her. "My hand," he said. He popped his palm on the lower curve of her ass and her shriek of pain was short and abrupt. Lovely. "Your ass. That's the agreement, right? Girl, we were both there last night when I lit you up. We."

She smiled and shivered when his slick fingers finally

slid over that little target. "I briefly considered starting off smaller and working our way up to Old Reliable but then I remembered. I'm an asshole."

"Sadist," she sighed as he pressed his finger into her. Her own hands flexed in response. "The correct word is sadist."

"Sadist. Asshole. They're interchangeable. Breathe, girl. Another." When he felt her body start to ease, he tucked into the first knuckle. "Pretty ass." He caressed his palm print before he began to work his way in until she made a startled sound. When he looked, she was gripping his pillow, her face pressed in to muffle those sexy little noises she made as he began to ease in and out.

Jesus. What had started as morning wood was a full-blown hard-on greedy to get in her. A year ago had anyone told him that Kate Jace Jennings would be spacing out in his bed, he'd have called them insane and offered to pay for their trip to rehab. The minute he had seen her though, it was like what Oz had said about her. His radar had pinged and he had snapped awake. Rolling out the day after his second sighting of her, meaning the first wasn't a fluke, had irritated him. Her fleeing had pissed him off because he had wanted to know why she was there.

The white band had been enough of a first box check of her being a sub, but he had wanted to know more. She had twigged his curiosity and imagination. The idea of tying up the daughter of Jace Jennings really should've cooled his jets. The girl had been a heartbreaking mess, so to suddenly see her as an adult had been a lightbulb moment.

Now here he was playing with her ass.

Life was crazy insane.

At least his was.

He reached for the black dildo and slowly pressed it into her pussy. She shuddered, her cry barely muffled by the pillow as he played. He eased the toy free of her completely and reached for the lube once more. "Now that you know it's not scary enormous…breathe in and relax."

"Oh, God," she moaned, her hands squeezing his pillow continuously. He heard her draw in, and as she exhaled, he slowly eased the toy through the tiny ring of muscle. Her back bowed, she cried out because his girl was not a quiet one when it came to sex, but eventually her muscles relaxed bit by bit until she was nice and full. "Pretty ass," he said again as he kissed where he had spanked, easing her so she was back on her heels.

Cupping under her chin, he tilted her head back. Her cheeks were flushed, her pupils dilated so there was only a small green rim left. He kissed her as he settled back on the bed. His cock was so hard it ached. He wished he had brought the clamps in from the bathroom because the image of her kneeling there with her face bright with arousal while her breasts were getting tortured hit all his buttons. "Eyes on me."

Her long lashes lifted and she looked at him, wetting her lips with the tip of her tongue. She was halfway there. He couldn't wait to get her to Edge and on that cross. "So, Katey Jay, you owe me a story." Running his fingers up his dick, she watched her, breath feathering out as she flattened her hands on her thighs. "So you're going to sit there and tell me all about the moment Katey Jay dipped into the submissive pool. Let me see your pretty eyes," he said when she closed them. "Shall I start you up?"

Her fingers flexed and he grinned slowly, well aware she was so far beyond start up that it was amazing to see. The knowledge that she trusted him was a blow to the gut. Not a lot, but just enough that she wasn't running from him any more. Just enough that she was letting him into her head, giving him glimpses of who she should've been but for life and two very shitty parents. A Kate with no ghosts in her eyes. A Kate with a feisty, bratty side. A Kate who trusted. Those small glimpses made him feel like a god damn superhero. Those small glimpses were fucking amazing.

"Once upon a time," he started, and his fingers wandered back down with her gaze tracking the movement, "there was a good girl named Kate and she had some baaaaaad thoughts." Her eyebrows rose and she peeked up at him from beneath her lashes, a grin appeared. "Tell the big, bad Doyle all about those baaaaad thoughts. In intimate detail."

"So," she flicked a quick little look his way and returned to watching his finger sliding up and down his cock, "you know that video you made?"

He blinked slowly as her words hit him like a two by four. "I made a lot of videos. All kinds."

She gasped, sitting up straight. "Liar!"

"Nothing but the truth. So perhaps you'd better get a bit more," he took in the sight of her, hot and bothered, kneeling between his legs, "explicit." He held up two fingers and parted them. When she shifted her legs open, the movement made her eyelids flicker thanks to her ass being bumped. "Which video?"

He wanted her to say the song. To voice it out loud.

"Other Side."

He remembered what she said, how she'd turn the volume off and totally get off on imagining it was her.

"The first time I saw I was sixteen…seventeen." She blushed and looked at his knee. "I had heard about it before. A video that controversial is going to be talked about. But I didn't really comprehend it until I was eighteen. Maybe I hadn't really paid attention before then. Truthfully the first time I saw it, it scared me. But it stuck."

"At me, Kate." He loved see her eyes as she sank deeper into her submission. The trust she gave him reflected in the green, and no lie, it hit all his buttons seeing that.

She nodded and met his gaze. "I don't know what I was looking for when I played the video. I watched. I really watched and I felt like you keep saying: like this switch was hit and I came…alive. The second time I watched it, I had to mute it. Everything just vanished. There was only…" She shrugged.

His voice was low and rough. Not so much because a teenage Kate had gone cruising through YouTube. That was…pretty high on the creep scale. "You told me you used to imagine it was you being topped by me." He released his grip, grabbed her arms and flipped her over so she was on her back. "When was the last time you watched it on silent, hand between your legs and wishing it was you on my cross?"

"Thursday before I went to the club," she whispered.

"Fuck," he moaned as he gazed down at her, his hand searching for the condom he had tossed out earlier, well aware he was going to end up in her. Finally he found it, tore it open and quickly sheathed himself. "Take it in."

"Take…why—"

She shouted when he pushed into her, snug from the dildo filling her ass. He caressed his hand over her forehead and fisted it in her hair, tilting her head back. When he moved within her, she released a half-cry, half-gasp sound he felt in his balls. "So are you insinuating I was, in a way, your first dom?"

A shudder moved through her as she rose to meet him, a shattered sound come from her as he glided over the hard penetration in her ass, nudging it. "Yes, Sir!"

"Take it in. Hold it," he demanded as he reached down and slowly dragged the artificial dick from her. A low moan came from her when he slid deep into her and reached over to set the toy on the nightstand. He felt the change in her body, felt the way it settled, the way she took the hard thrusts.

Simmer down, Kolemann.

He paused and gazed down at her. He ran his thumb over her mouth, feeling the softness of her lips. Leaning down, he kissed her. Sliding his hand under her ass, he eased them so she was above him. A soft gasp and then she was riding him, his fingers sliding along the curve of her hip, up to a breast. Her brown hair tumbled forward as she braced her hands on his stomach. The morning sun seemed to hit her at some interesting angles. His fingers combed into her hair and he drew her down to get to her mouth. "Finish that sentence, Kate. There was only what? Tell me."

Her eyes were closed and he gave a tug on her hair until she was looking at him. "You," she whispered.

He gazed into her eyes that were fogged with passion but empty of ghosts. For now. They'd come back. Ghosts haunted. For now though, it was all Kate. Talk about an intoxicating feeling. "Is that why you fled the first time you saw me in the club?"

"Yes."

"I'm going to put you on your back and then I'm going to fuck the hell out of you."

She sucked in her breath and her eyelids flickered close. "Yes please, Sir."

He flipped her to her back, caught her under her knees and slammed deep into her. She cried out, bucking up into him, welcoming him into her. "Let's bring some of those pain screams into play."

"Oh. God."

"We both know he's not here right now." Lowering his head he bit the inside of her breast hard enough to make her sing with pain. Beautiful. Every good bass beat needed a melody, any halfway decent musician knew that. He was more than halfway decent and he played her body expertly. Doyle found every spot that made her scream, made her come.

Made her his.

"Yo, D! Just a warning, don't come out naked."

Kate's eyes snapped open at the familiar deep voice that shouted through the door.

"Fuck." Doyle didn't move, his fingers gently sliding over her back. "Unexpected company."

Had he heard? She looked at the door then at Doyle. The warning implied that he had totally heard them having sex. "What do we do?"

His dark eyes looked at her while one inked shoulder shrugged. "Don't go out naked." He untangled himself from beneath her and walked over to where his jeans were. She watched him drag them up without bothering with his underwear. He grabbed his shirt, then her ankles, and pulled her down the bed, a surprised yelp coming from her.

"This is pretty," he said, rubbing his knuckles lightly over the marks he had put on her. "While Max is one of the few I can tolerate, he doesn't get to see them. So you put this on and I'm going to find your panties because he gets no sneaky looks either."

"See?"

Doyle went still at her question and braced his fists by her hips, getting in her face. "I'm not a fan of dirty little secrets."

"But I'm Jace's…" her voice faded away as he caught her wrists and pulled her up so she was sitting. He dragged the shirt over her head and she had the choice of putting her arms through the sleeves or looking stupid. She put her arms through her sleeves.

"What did you say earlier, girl?"

She wet her lips as she met his hard stare. The girl part told her things were about to either get kinky or serious. She was going for the latter. Focusing on the sleeve of tattoos on his right arm, she rubbed her thumb over a rather gruesome image. He caught her chin and made her look at him, waiting for her to answer. A lot was said earlier.

"The only ones with power and control over you are you and me."

"I didn't say that exactly."

A black eyebrow arched up but she nodded. Hard to argue with the truth.

"How's you hiding in my bedroom because Max is out there you holding onto that? I'm calling bullshit on that because you're still giving Jace way more power than he ever deserved." He pushed upright and walked out of the bedroom.

Kate sat there and crossed her legs. The low murmur of male voices drifted to her. Jace sure as hell wouldn't care who she was in bed with so why would anyone else? She plucked at the bottom of her shirt as she thought.

She could hide in here as Doyle had said, or she could take a deep breath, be an adult and own the fact that since Friday night, the man had been inside her. She had a feeling hiding wouldn't end well for her. Exhaling softly, she slipped on her panties and jeans because somehow facing Max without either made her feel vulnerable. She ran her fingers over her stomach and felt all the sore spots Doyle had put on her. Bites and bruises. Knowing they were there made her feel light-headed in a good way. Since she'd like future marks, she shook the nerves out of her hands and left the safety of his bedroom.

She followed the two voices into the kitchen: Doyle's deep one and Max's low, raspy one. Doyle was setting ingredients on the island while Max was lighting a cigarette while he talked. "Fuck, I dunno, man. This shit is getting old."

She stopped in the doorway and rubbed her foot on the back of her calf. Maximillian Jones was a bit older than Doyle and hadn't been one of the original band members. He had come in just before their second album when the other guy, Eps, had wound up in jail. She found out a lot on the internet when it came to knowing about the band. Who was going to tell her? Jace?

Doyle didn't respond but instead began to butcher a green pepper.

"It's a god damn mess," Max said as he blew smoke out, bracing his hands on the island. "What…the fuck?"

She blushed when he spotted her. Staring. Doyle winked at her, making her smile.

"Jesus, D. Seriously? She's what? How old are you again?"

"Old enough," Doyle said cutting off his band mate. "You like eggs?"

"I like eggs," she said. Doyle Kole was making her breakfast. How crazy was that? "Hi, Max."

"Fuck, Doyle."

"Yes, she did," Doyle said as he turned his attention to breakfast. She tugged on the bottom of his shirt as Max continued to stare, his cigarette forgotten. "Stop making her uncomfortable and blink. Come help me, girl."

Did he have any idea what it did to her when he called her that? Maybe she should be offended, but she wasn't. She had witnessed too many doms calling their subs that and to have him call her that left her feeling aglow. "What do you want me to do?" When she walked over to him, he grabbed her by the waist and lifted her onto the smooth marble.

"You're doing it." He tapped her thigh with the back of his chef's knife and she stared at the stainless steel, then at him. His grin was dangerous and she decided it was a good thing Max hadn't seen it. "Noted," he murmured as he resumed chopping.

Oh hell, she thought, trying to calm her racing heart.

"This is all kinds of fucked up," Max said as he sucked on his cigarette. "Do you have any idea what he does?"

The knife paused briefly before it resumed its steady rhythm. "He's the drummer. Right?" This time Doyle stopped cutting and she could feel him staring at her with an intensity completely at odds with the frown on Max's face. She had always thought of Max as the nice one. He didn't drink, he didn't do drugs. His addiction was weddings. She couldn't even remember what wife number he was on now. She'd Google when she got home.

She picked up a slice of pepper and chewed on it while she looked at Max, giving him her most innocent eyes. What he does? What the heck did that mean?

"Aside from that."

"He writes the music with Carl too. Right?" The knife made a soft click and when she glanced at Doyle, she saw he had laid the knife down and stood with his hands braced on the sleek grey surface, watching her. "Right? That's what you do?"

"God damn it," Max snapped out. "I mean fucking, Kate."

"Oooooh." She nibbled on her vegetable, enjoying the sweet tart kick to it. "You do things?" The corners of his eyes crinkled but his face had this intenseness to it, his nearly black eyes were even darker and his mouth was in a flat line.

"He doesn't fuck normal, Kate."

This was fun. "So...like abnormal? Abnormal how? I saw that a kind of snail inseminates through the neck. You don't fuck necks, do you? Because that's just...not normal."

She swung her feet, drumming her heels on the door beneath her as she picked up another slice of pepper.

"God damn it," Max now shouted. "He's into kink,

Kate. The kind that causes pain. With whips and shit."

"Oh," she said quietly. "That. Are these from the market on Granville? They're amazing. What?"

Doyle moved, pushing her legs open so he could stand between them. "Remember when I said the day you trusted enough to brat out would be fucking fantastic and would lead to fantastic fucking?"

She nodded once.

He caught her, tossed her over her shoulder, and then carried her out of the kitchen, Max staring at them with his mouth open. "Now's a good time to fuck off, Max."

Kate - 2003

It was so innocent and innocuous, but standing by her bed she felt nauseous and terrified. As scared as she had been when her mother had been in her chair, the needle in her arm and the stink of death in the small trailer. As scared as she had been when the cops showed up and she had cowardly hid in her spot, tears of fear and heartache sliding to the floor. As scared as when she had come home and there was nothing.

Terror clung to her as she stared at the hockey jersey carefully laid out on her bed, the arms neatly folded in an almost lewd fashion. She felt dizzy when she saw the NO. where names went and the giant one smack dab in the middle of the back.

"You taste sweet, my pretty little No One. I bet you taste sweet all over."

Resting at the bottom was a simple note. She clamped her hands over her mouth as the sob strangled there. She actually tightened her thighs, afraid she was going pee down her leg and over the sock of her uniform. *Danger, danger, danger.*

Her knees buckled and she collapsed to the floor. She did what she always did when there was danger or a threat. She slid under her bed, craving the darkness and wishing there was the plywood door she could wedge in place. Just in case.

Just in case.

She pressed her body up against the pictures taped there. As if the glossy images from the magazines could save her. As if he would save her. *No one. No one.* Her uniform clung to skin turned clammy. Had he been in her room? *Danger, danger, danger.*

No one.

No. One.

Number 1.

Happy birthday, No One.

Happy birthday, Kate.

Chapter 11

KATE WAS PRETTY sure she was the only one who used the storage room. Jace wasn't the type to hold onto things. Carefully wrapped in protective padding was her beloved white desk, and the matching chair was wrapped in its own layers and lay on the top. One day, when she had her own space, she would bring it out of this basement. There was a cedar armoire that held her favorite pieces of clothing. Her first uniform for school, the outfit she had worn when she had met Jace, her dress from the first Christmas and way too many concert tees for Cyanide that were of various ages. Sometimes she felt like a stalker in her own life when she saw the shirts from all the tours. Shows she hadn't seen but had wanted the mementos for the very reason that they were a part of Jace's life.

She had kept everything. School assignments, articles and magazines from when her existence had broken in the news. She had stopped hoarding food and had resorted to hoarding pieces of this life. Even now, years later, she justified holding onto everything with the simple reason that for one terrifying moment she had lost everything.

She wished she didn't have this urge to keep items from crucial moments in her life, because then things wouldn't be tangible for her. The box shoved under the blanket draped over her desk was very tangible.

Wiping her damp palms on the thighs of her jeans, Kate stared at her covered desk, well aware of what was buried under its shadows. She would have left it alone but for Doyle. Not that he knew that the box even existed, but talking about her past made her want to confront the dragon. A small part of her wanted to set it on fire and forget the box ever existed, to let it go.

A larger part of her wanted to thrust the contents at someone else with the whispered hope that they'd be able to make everything better. She wanted to unload it all. Until Doyle had brought it up, she hadn't realized how tired she was of carrying this around. Not that she ever had anyone to show her past. Counseling had been good but she hadn't felt safe to give all. Within a short week, Doyle had made her feel safe.

That was the thought that made her exhale the breath she felt strangling in her chest. She sank to her knees to flip the grey blanket back and reach back until her fingers touched the box. It felt cold to her, colder than the concrete floor. Dragging it free, she stared at the massive layers of tape covering the flaps. Keeping the dragon in.

All her boxes on the shelves were labeled: school work, books, Cyanide. This box had nothing on it. A label wasn't necessary. She had sealed it with a savage desperation, almost using an entire roll of packing tape. Pushing the box aside, she eased the blanket back down, smoothing it to protect the desk.

Not until Kate approached the partially open door,

did she hear low, deep voices and she winced at the realization that Jace was home. Usually she actively sought him out when they were both in the house. With the chill spreading through her because of the box, she felt too vulnerable to deal with the man who still didn't know what to do with her. She wasn't that complicated. Setting the box down long enough to lock the door behind her, Kate's steps slowed even more when she realized what the topic of conversation was about.

Or rather who.

"You sure you don't want to share with the class who you're fucking?" There was a slippery, snide tone to Anderson Reeve's voice, a cruelty that held barbs. Her numb fingers gripped the edge of her box.

"It doesn't matter," a familiar voice rumbled out and she looked down at the box of hell she was holding, not quite sure how she felt about that sentence. A sharp sensation was crawling under her skin.

"Well then." Anderson wasn't a nice person, especially when he was using, as if all the poisons inside him made him feel like he had to spread that toxicity. "Share."

"No."

"Why are we discussing D's latest fuck toy?"

She shut her eyes as Jace's voice clawed through her. She thought she heard Max softly curse.

"Because it's a very interesting fuck toy."

Fuck toy. The words bounced around her head, hammering at her. She told herself he didn't know he was referring to his daughter as his band mate's fuck toy. Not that he'd likely care. She saw herself standing in this very basement, stuttering and stammering at him, looking for him to step up and be her dad. Instead he hadn't cared.

And there was this box.

This fucking box and everything it held. This box she was too scared to hold onto but too afraid to get rid of. The dark had always been a safe place for her and as she stood in the unlit, seldom used exercise room, it turned on her.

She wanted to hear that she wasn't a fuck toy, that she was something…someone.

This house, she thought as she held her breath, waiting. This house of nightmares and shadows hungry to devour her up. *Stop them, stop them.* Defend. Just once… just once she wanted to not feel alone in this god damn house that was supposed to have been a safe place.

Always, always wanting.

"We're here to work," her dom snapped out, "not discuss my fuck life."

There it was.

Or wasn't.

The chill from the box was sliding up her arms until she was afraid of dropping it. The weight of it shifted until she swore it was trying to push her into the ground, bury her. All because she had wanted to not carry the burden of it, because she had wanted to trust him with *all* of it. Because she had wanted to trust him. Period. *Always wanting.*

"Music. Album. Write," Carl said. "I do not want to hear about D's kink."

"But it's gotten so interesting," Anderson drawled, dragging the word interesting out like he was torturing it. "Hasn't it, D?"

"Stop talking," Max muttered under his breath.

Considering he had probably been the one to tell

Anderson, she thought that was a bit hypocritical.

"D's fuck toy doesn't matter. The music does. Let's do this shit."

She really wanted them to stop referring to her as a fuck toy. She wanted Doyle to stop them. She needed him to. Kate listened, waited.

What she got was "Is it just me or is this break utter shit?"

She really needed that one percent glimmer of hope to just give up and die. There was the rustle of paper.

Her throat felt tight and there was a burning in her jaw that was at odds with the chill in her hands.

She could, she realize, stand in the dark until they were done. All she wanted, however, was to get out. Out of this god damn house where she was inconsequential, where she was a fuck toy, where she was no one. This world. This toxic, horrible world.

He was right.

This wasn't her world, because she couldn't conform to it. She was tired. So tired of dredging it alone in this world. Exhaling slowly, she let it go. Let it die in the shadows of Jace Jennings' exercise room.

"Red," she whispered, and opened her eyes. Enough. *Enough, Kate.* That's what he said: when it hurt or became too much, she had the power. She had the power to stop it from hurting or overwhelming her. Tightening her fingers on the side edges of the box, she made herself step out of the dark.

The stairs were situated on the other side of the sectional sofa were the band was. It was a familiar set up. Carl and Max with their guitars, Jace sprawled along the entire middle section of the horseshoe-shaped couch, while

Anderson looked like a child who was about to have a massive tantrum because nobody was paying attention to him as he smoked a cigarette. Doyle sat on a cajón drum box, his legs spread while he quietly drummed his fingers on the edge as he looked at the music on the table.

She was always surprised the wooden box held him up because he made it look small and fragile. He didn't bring his drums here, not since a drunk Anderson had grabbed one of the snare drums and threw it into the television. Anderson was why they now wrote out here instead of in Jace's music room. Had to protect the important things.

"Fuck." Max was staring at her. His gaze flicked from her to Doyle to the room she had just emerged from.

The light, steady tapping stopped and she made herself look at Doyle. *Enough, Kate. This fuck toy says what?* "Red," she told him. Clutching her box, she made herself go up the curved stairs. She was not going to cry in this house anymore.

She needed to put this box down, find someplace new to store it. She refused to take it back to her studio, refused to have it taint her haven. She also didn't want it where she slept. That gave her nowhere.

She shouldn't have come for it.

She should have left it in the dark, buried in the storage room. Leave it in this house.

"Kate–"

"Red. Didn't you say a good dom listened, observed?" She had to set the box down to open the door to the garage and there was relief at not touching it. Once she had the door open, she hit the button for the far garage door. Jace's fancy sports car and SUV took up the two main spots, but she got the last one. Well, not her. Usually whatever girl was currently living in his bed, but since there was nobody, she had been able to use the garage. A rarity.

The box. She could not leave the box. As much as she wanted too, she couldn't. Grabbing it, she looked at Doyle, who looked irritated. Too bad. She was bleeding.

She was tired of it.

"You were right. This isn't my world. I don't want it anymore. So…red." She wanted to scream it at him but that required far more than she was capable of.

"What do you think happened down there?"

"I think my dom let them call me a fuck toy. That's what I think happened down there." *Red.* Like the blood spilling from thin scars. *Red.*

She kicked the door shut and the bang wasn't as satisfying as it should've been. She shoved the box into her trunk before she slid into the driver's seat. Her hands were shaking as she gripped the steering wheel, lowering her head down. Tired. She was so tired of this happening to her.

"Red, Kate. Red."

Kate - 2003

There was no rhyme or reason to when a present would show up on her bed. Sometimes a week would go by, maybe two. Or for three days she'd come home to find something on her bed. Locking her door didn't help. She'd come home and there would be an envelope that said *Pretty Little No One* on it and inside would be a ticket to a movie or a play or a hockey game. Sometimes it was a gift card or a note. Nothing was signed but she knew. She knew.

She stared at the envelope propped against her pillow and her stomach began to hurt. Her knotted ribbon had finally disintegrated. She had found a pretty yellow one that had come wrapped around a present for Natalie, her half-sister. Since it had been in the trash, she had considered it fair game. The extra length was curled up in the top drawer of her dresser along with other ribbons she had salvaged.

Shaelynn and the baby were gone. Apparently Shaelynn had realized that Jace had no desire to be a father to her daughter. The fight had been loud and violent. The next day Shaelynn and Natalie were gone, along with all the pretty presents. It was nice to not have Shaelynn screaming all the time, but weird to be in a house where it was just her, Jace and the nanny, who used to live downstairs but was currently in Jace's bed.

Sandra had decided Kate needed someone to look after her. Mostly though she had wanted to be Jace's lover. She sure didn't take care of Kate. At twelve, Kate really didn't need anyone to babysit her. Actually, she never had.

Self-reliant. That's what her teacher had said she was. She liked that word.

Now, though, she didn't feel very self-reliant. She picked up the envelope and whatever was in it rattled, slithering from one corner to the next. Flipping up the flap she stared at the gold necklace inside. A simple chain with a charm on it. Her stomach cramped when she saw it was a number one. Dropping the latest present, she stumbled back from her bed.

For a short time, Kate had felt safe in her bedroom.

There were walls, a comfortable bed. She had a pile of money hidden because at odd times she'd find an envelope filled with money tossed on her bed. Her birthday, Christmas. Two thousand dollars each time. What she'd do with two thousand dollars every time, she didn't know. Now though, she wanted to grab all her money and run back to the trailer park.

Since her birthday and the hockey jersey, Kate had begun stockpiling cans under her bed again.

Twisting the bright new knot, Kate fled the trap that was her bedroom. She stumbled down the curving stairs because Jace liked circles. The lights that hung down the curving staircase from the top floor to the basement were circles. The bar in the basement was round, his shower was round, his office was round. He even had a tattoo of joined circles around his biceps. The sound of music came from the basement and she continued down the round staircase, only to stop when she saw Jace.

He sat on the curved couch, his guitar in place while he sipped from a bottle of beer. It was weird to see him alone. No band members, no groupies, no friends. She twisted and squeezed a knot as she approached the sectional on her tip toes. Folding her arms on the back of the black leather, she watched him play and sing.

When he sang, he made her heart feel tight and funny. She didn't always understand what he was singing about but she understood the passion and love in his voice. He loved to sing. He was really, really good at it.

This man was her father.

The thought came at the oddest times, flooding her with an alien feeling because she never called him Dad. Not even in her head. He was Jace. Pressing her mouth against her forearm, she got lost in the song. In the power of it. Jace was a horrible father, even she had realized this in six months of living here, but he was an amazing musician.

"Fuck. Damn it." He flexed out his hand and made a note on the paper sitting on the round table. He looked up and spotted her watching. A frown appeared as if he struggled to remember who she was and why she was here.

Kate, she thought to herself. *I'm Kate.*

"What?" He sounded impatient, like she was inconveniencing him. *I'm Kate. I'm yours.*

"I—" She pinched skin on her wrist, she was turning the knot so much. Struggling to find the words, he became impatient and returned to the music. "There's this guy," she said. He sighed and slapped his hands over the strings, cutting the music off. "He keeps…he…he…" Tears burned as she struggled. In her head it was all there. He kept putting presents on her bed, he scared her, he had kissed her at the New Year's Eve party in a way no one should kiss a child, he scared her so much.

"This boy is bugging you?"

She nodded.

"Tell him to piss off."

"But—" Jace turned is attention back to the music, done with her. *He's not a boy*, she finished in her head.

Chapter 12

FINDING ONE WOMAN should not have been this hard. Yes, there were over half a million people in the city, but finding Kate should've been a lot easier. Her apartment had been treacherous. Her roommates were something else. It was hard to imagine his sweet girl living with those two. They were walking vaginas. Groupies. Immaterial. After that he had been at a loss.

He had even checked the penthouse though it had been empty. Jace was zero help so he hadn't even bothered. After that who was there to call? He didn't know her friends. He knew dick all. Except that he had hurt her. Unintentionally.

"You mind-fuck, Doyle," Oz said, "you don't fuck with her mind. Maybe you should–"

"Maybe you should not finish that sentence. I fucked up. I get it."

His friend went quiet for a few seconds. "Maybe I should finish it. Are you sure pursuing this is the right thing to do? Not for you, for her. You're the one who said she was fragile."

Had he? He couldn't remember. Impatiently, he tapped his thumb on the leather wrapped steering wheel.

His gaze landed on the black ring that had one day been waiting for him at the club just before he had left on tour. It was a deceptively simple design. He remembered the text where she confessed she had made the ring for him. Kate wasn't one to easily give up her secrets.

She clutched them tight. So for her to have shared even that tiny nugget had been rare. Smoothing his index finger along the band, he remembered the slack from the others at him wearing the ring. He wasn't a jewelry kind of guy. Fuck, he hadn't even worn his wedding ring. Not because he hadn't loved Claire and he had planned on fucking around on her, it just wasn't his thing. Had it been an issue? He couldn't remember. He did know Oz wore his. Doyle also knew he hadn't taken Kate's ring off since he had slid it on.

Hello, asshole, here's an obvious statement.

"Your wife was the one who told me she was stronger than she realized." He snatched up his phone and opened up the text conversation that had been going with Kate pretty steadily until today. He thumbed through random snippets: some clean, some very much not clean. Fun was telling her what to do and making her text back as he made her touch herself. She wasn't allowed to fix typos. There were a lot of typos.

Doyle found what he was looking for, halting the scrolling to look at the photo, at her words when she told him this was Kate's world. He watched the video. Nothing about the space said workshop or warehouse. Rental? Doubtful. She had the carcasses of guitars on walls. So that meant somewhere in the city, there was something with Kate's name on it. Someone would've helped her with the legalities. Someone like– "I gotta go." He disconnected the call, cutting his friend off in mid-word.

Starting the engine, he told his hands-free to call Charlie.

"How goes the work session?" Their manager never joined them. He had a low tolerance for bullshit.

"No one's dead. Kate Jennings."

"I'm acquainted with her."

Dick. "Where is she set up?"

"Is this an emergency?"

Her green eyes filled with pain and something broken. Something that had felt a lot like her fragile trust. *"I think my dom let them call me a fuck toy. That's what I think happened down there."*

Hell yes, this was a fucking emergency. "Yes."

His manager hesitated. Charles rattled off the apartment where the venus flytrap vaginas were. "No, I don't want that shitty apartment. I want to know where she's set up."

"Doyle, I can't in good conscience–"

"It's been a while since I threw down. I'm a little rusty, and I'm sober, but it shouldn't be that hard to remember."

"Are you threatening me with throwing a tantrum?"

"Well, I know how much you like cleaning up after us, Charles. It's just a matter of how big a mess I make. You have a fondness for having to bail us out of jail, don't you?"

"God damn it, Doyle. You're an asshole."

"How hard is it to clean up a mess when it hits Twitter? This wasn't around for me before. Big and messy. Maybe someone accidentally gets hurt." Jesus. He was not rocking sanity at all. "Kate. Jennings. Voila, no shit storm."

"Fucker." He gave an address.

"Always a pleasure, Charlie." He hung up as he fed her location to the GPS. Not even his blackmail was a big of mess to clean up as this. Trust was fragile. Especially with someone who rarely experienced it. Throw in the mind-fuck world of her submission, and things could get extremely sticky. He knew better.

Assholes like Anderson were manipulative jack-offs. Unhappy with their lives, they had to make everyone else miserable. The mind-fuck had caught him by surprise. Usually he was able to handle the bassist's bullshit, but that it had been Kate had blindsided him. How Anderson knew wasn't the point. Maybe he had come into the penthouse when they had been scening, maybe he had actually known who she had been at the party. The how wasn't important.

He had beaten the shit out of Anderson years ago when he had said something about Claire. Doyle had loved Claire. She had been his fiancée and his submissive. One snide comment and he had put his band mate in the floor. Anderson wasn't a fighter. Even blitzed out of his brain, Doyle had put the beat down on him. He was bigger, stronger, and he knew how to cause pain. He enjoyed it.

But Kate.

That had been different. All kinds of different.

Her building was in a newly trendy area where old warehouses were being renovated into lofts, condos and office space. Getting in was surprisingly easy. All it took was an autograph on a guy's arm and a selfie picture that he tweeted out to the world.

Someone needed better security.

The large warehouse was pretty much split in half, with four lofts on one side and two levels of condos on another. He went left until he reached the last door. Knocking beneath the spy hole, he looked around. The place still had a warehouse feeling, with concrete cinder blocks making up the wall and heavy doors announcing the personal spaces. The light above the door looked like it belonged on the exterior and nothing that he had seen so far screamed Kate.

Nothing but the face that appeared in the door cracked open.

She looked pale, with bruising under her eyes, making the green look darker. There was something familiar on her face; he had just never seen it because of him. Usually it was her stellar father who gave her a haunted look. God damn it. He hated seeing it directed at him.

He braced his hand on the doorframe above her head because he wanted to grab her. The frame was easier and safer. He had damaged something fragile today.

"I broke Anderson's jaw when he called Claire a submissive cunt. I'd love to be honorable and say it was only one hit, but I took him to the floor and tried to introduce his nose to the floor via the back of his skull. We had a show, he wound up in surgery with his jaw wired in place and a buddy of Carl's had to fill in for the rest of the tour because Anderson got hooked on pain meds that he would blend into milkshakes laced with booze. Charlie made me pay for Anderson's hospital bills and attend some anger management courses. Flash forward fifteen years."

Reaching out, he brushed her bangs out of her eyes and a tiny flinch moved through her. Fuck. *You haven't earned the right to touch her there, Kolemann.* "Fifteen years later," he said as he lowered his hand. "I'm clean, I've got fifteen more years of muscle and he's rotting from the inside out. That's not why I didn't turn Jace's white carpet red."

"Didn't want to pay his medical bills?"

"There are few times when life has surprised me with an upper cut. A pop to the chin that leaves you standing there, shaking your head as your ears ring. I can count them on one hand in the past fifteen years." His thumb pointed up. "Finding Claire in bed with Jace. Seeing you in Edge," his index finger aimed at the door followed by his middle finger, "and the cold-blooded rage I felt in Jace's basement. I don't like my bandmates. Maybe Max. I don't even remotely respect them. We're a small group of selfish assholes who lost sight of why we started this band long ago. We waste our talent and harm those we're supposed to love the most. Why anyone buys our albums and comes to concerts is beyond me. We're sliding into mediocrity and that fucking drives me nuts."

"What does that have to do with me?"

Everything. He rested his head on his arm as he gazed down at her. "I wanted to end him, Katey. I talk about beating the shit out of Jace because he's a total fuck up as a human being. I didn't even take a swing at your father when I came home to find him nailing my wife. I walked out. I turned around and walked away. But Anderson." He took a deep breath and held it, trying to smother that rage that built up remembering the man's face as he talked about Kate. His Kate. His sweet girl who had just been emerging from a lifetime of hurt. "I am not exaggerating when I say I wanted to end him. I could. I grew up on the streets. I was a big, strong kid filled with a lot of anger. He grew up the spoiled, pampered son of a politician. I learned to fight in back alleys and he learned to snort shit up his nose. I lift weights and run every day, because if I don't, I don't have the strength and stamina to get through a show. He still puts shit up his nose. For fun I take crops, whips and straps to pretty submissives and can beat on one for a long time. For fun he puts shit up his nose.

"Ending him wouldn't be hard. One good hit and he's out. But it wouldn't be one hit. It wouldn't even have been the rage-filled beating I gave him over Claire. He wouldn't just hurt, I'd make him beg. I'd draw it out. We both know I'm good at drawing out pain. Just thinking about it makes me want to go back and put that junkie in the ground."

"You didn't say anything, Doyle. Nothing. You went to work like he said he didn't like your shirt."

She was torturing the hell out of her bracelet. She hadn't done that, he realized, since the night of the party. There had been the usual fiddling with it, but nothing like the twisting and rolling of one knot over and over again. Reaching down, he pressed his finger against hers, halting the movement because she was catching skin and turning it pink.

He rubbed his fingertip over the small hurt she had inflicted. "I could say that he's a lot like a wasp and that engaging with him only makes things worse, which is true."

"But?"

"But mostly I was too busy trying to deal with the rage. Calm my shit before I did something I couldn't take back. Look what I did, eh? Did something I can't take back." He rolled one of the knots between his fingers. The leather was smooth and worn from countless touches from her. "The irony of protecting the asshole is not lost on me. In short, I fucked up."

Since she hadn't pulled her hand away, which he took as progress, Doyle touched the small bruises that were fading. He liked this bracelet, but he made a mental note on the amount of pressure to put on it.

"I don't know if I can forgive you," she said quietly, watching his finger touch each mark he had put there.

"I don't want you to."

Surprise made her look up. "I don't want this to fade for either of us like these little dots are." Breaking points needed to be remembered. "Will you show me your world, Katey Jay?"

She blinked slowly, clearly not expecting the question. She looked over her shoulder into the space as if seeking permission. He half expected her to say no, but a tiny jerk of her head made his body relax for the first time all afternoon. When she opened the door, he felt lucky. Very lucky. This could've gone the other way.

Stepping inside, the first thing he saw was the wall of guitars. The video scan didn't quite prepare him for how many she had. "Jesus, Kate. Where did you get all of this?"

She tucked her hair behind her ear as she followed his gaze. "Around."

The rest of the space was just as impressive. Two pianos picked apart faced each other as if comparing war wounds. "So, which key made my ring?"

She ran her finger over an empty space. "D sharp."

"Funny girl."

"How did you know I gave it to you?"

"That was Jace's guitar. Do you know how much those go for now that he doesn't play?"

She nodded. He gave everything a more thorough look. Plucking up a black drum stick that he knew he had once held, he twirled it through his fingers. There weren't just garage finds in this place. There was history. The stairs were against one wall and beneath the upper floor was the kitchen. Curiosity took him upstairs to see some lethal looking tools. There was a shit ton of expensive items in here. All it took was one asshole to figure out where she was and pick this place clean.

He began to tap the drum stick against his thigh as he went back downstairs and finally headed to the tables. "Jesus, Katey." Draped around a faceless head, the necklace was intricate, made up of thin metal strings that looked like they had come from one of the violins. She had somehow managed to recreate the illusion of the F-holes in the negative while gemstone notes danced over the wires.

He looked from the necklace to Kate, then back. Sheet music was tacked up on the wall.

"The tough part," she said as she reached out to adjust the impressive piece, "is making it look like the music when it lies on the body and when it lays flat. She wanted her husband to literally play the music off her. It's taken a long time, but it's going to open a lot of doors for me. One, the money is insane. Two, the exposure. The strings actually came from his violin and we spent a lot of time debating what gems to use."

"What if he hates it?"

"He won't."

The self-confidence made him study her. She hadn't lied, he realized. This really was her world. "Who's the client?"

"Jens Homstead. He once played with the Royal Philharmonic. He's now one of their conductors."

"How the hell did the daughter of a Canadian rocker hook up with a conductor in England?"

She shrugged. "Luck."

"Kate. Luck is finding five bucks on the ground. This is impressive, girl. This is truly impressive." On the other table there was a sketchpad with a spider web. Something about it was familiar. Instead of asking, he turned and braced his hands on the drawing table's edge. "Look at what you've done." She shrugged, but he saw her small, pleased smile even as she blushed.

Reaching out, he grabbed her hand and walked over to the twin bed that was where a kitchen table should be. A place to crash if she was up late working. He barely fit, especially when he drew her down so she was snuggled up against him. Tucking one arm behind his head, he gazed at her workshop.

There was a slight tension to her that hadn't been there for a while. He had done that. "Breathe," he told her as he gazed at her wall of stringed instruments in various states of dissection. "Let's just lie here and gaze at your world. For the record, you're not a fuck toy. A fuck toy is what I happily use on you. Claire was right." Glancing at her, he saw her head rested on his chest as she too looked at what she was creating.

Kate lifted her head, her forehead crinkling as she frowned. "About what?"

"You're stronger than you know you are. You're doing this all on your own and you let me in to see it."

"I already showed you it."

"No. You gave me a peek." Impulsively, he kissed the tip of her nose. A tiny smile escaped from her before she lowered her head. He didn't know what he said, but he felt the muscles relax. "Wanna see mine?"

What the hell? What? He tried to process what had come out of his month. His world was on a small Gulf Island where his girls randomly popped by whenever they wanted. It was not a place he invited a lot of people. Just his friends, no bands, no subbies from the club, nobody casual.

But hadn't he just realized that she wasn't somebody casual? That she wasn't just a girl from the club?

"Yes," Kate answered quietly. "I'd love to."

This time he was the one to relax.

Kate - 2003

There was going to be another party. A big one. Twisting her knot, she watched as the catering team set up. A deejay was taking up a wall in the living room while all kinds of lights were put in place. She watched it all unfold. It was Jace's birthday and he was thirty. Unlike at Christmas, there was no camera crew recording all of this. She had left his present in his office because she hadn't seen him for a few days. That everything was going on was the only hint that something was happening here.

It was hard to get a present for a man who could buy anything in the world. She was twelve so it wasn't like she could find a drug dealer to get him drugs, which he would probably appreciate more than the vintage poster she had found of one of his favorite musicians.

The shine of Jace Jennings had faded a long time ago. The dream of a father had turned to ashes but there was still that one percent chance of hope. Hope that he'd suddenly realize that he had this daughter and she wasn't the worst thing to ever happen to him. Hope that one day he'd remember her birthday. Hope that he'd just see her.

That one percent was killing her.

The nanny was gone, replaced by some model who didn't look that much older than Kate. Sometimes she envied Shaelynn and Sandy, the former nanny. At least they got their one percent smashed to dust and were able to leave. She lived here and that one percent refused to die.

A bartender was setting up right in front of the front doors. There were even waitresses in skimpy uniforms who would be serving drinks. Probably sex.

Unlike the New Year's Eve party, Kate wasn't going to go looking for Jace. The presents from the man had escalated so now that every time she came home from school, there was a present waiting for her. Her room was no longer safe to her. Nightmares had her sleeping under her bed and if anyone noticed how perfectly her bed was made the next day, no one cared.

She felt lost and alone in this house. She had tried to talk to Jace a couple of times, but it never went well. She was terrified *he* would be here tonight and so she needed a better hiding place than her bedroom, because he could get in there. Someplace no one was allowed to go. But she needed to go now before it was too late. She had a key. She needed some food so she raided the pantry and ran downstairs. Sneaking the key from Jace's keys had been the most terrifying moment of her life. A stranger she didn't know scurried by, readying the basement. The bar down here was fully stocked and two bartenders were getting everything organized.

Her stomach hurt as she waited. She darted to the door, slipped the key in and snuck into the room.

This was the one room Jace had forbade her to go into. Not even with him. This was sacred. Once she had the door locked and the key in her pocket, she turned on the light and stared at this sanctuary for her father.

Guitars hung on the wall, along with framed gold and platinum albums. Wiping her sweaty palms on her jeans, she walked along the wall, looking at the history of Cyanide. Album covers, pictures of Jace with other stars. Her A computer was set up and there was even a micro-phone. Jace's music room.

She moved the stool in front of a picture of Jace when he was young, opened her bag of chips and nibbled, gaz-ing at him. She wished he loved her. She wished he liked her. Because she had all this love inside her for him and he didn't want it. Like Mom.

Kate couldn't hear anything through the walls. She napped on the leather couch, she touched the guitars, she even stole a guitar pick that sat forgotten on a table. She curled up on the couch and fell asleep, wishing that her life was different. Just a bit different. Not a lot. Be-cause she wasn't living in a trailer where there was a chill through the window above where she slept, she didn't have to worry about food. She just wished that Jace loved her.

One percent. It was killer.

When she woke up, her watch said it was five and she tidied up, erasing her presence. She snuck out and saw the bartenders were gone, though some people were still here, passed out in various states of undress. The house looked like a tornado had ripped through it. Bottles and glasses were everywhere, someone's shoes. A bra was dangling from the round lights that hung down the stairs. There was even a woman, naked on the stairs, her bare bum sticking up as she snored.

On her toes, Kate went up to her bedroom and was relieved to see it was still locked. Once she was in her room, she leaned against the door. Safe. Now she just had to get Jace's key back to him. Shoving the garbage from her snacks into the garbage can in the bathroom, Kate turned.

"Hello, Pretty little No One."

Chapter 13

KATE TUCKED HER hair behind her ear as she gazed around. The house was a lifestyle away from both Jace's over the top house and the penthouse. It was a simple two-storey built for a guy who liked open space. The main floor was open with the deck facing the water. Kate looked at him and then at the living room. He folded his arms over his chest and watched her explore. Her fingers brushed over the fireplace made of river rock. There was no glossy black marble like in Jace's, no stark modern lines like the penthouse.

"It's so…" She pushed open the sliding door to the deck and rested her forearms on the railing. He followed her out. A dog could be heard barking and a girl's laughter drifted through the trees. The view, though. The Strait of Georgia was right there, his grass bleeding into a rocky beach. One of the things she loved about living in Vancouver was the water. She loved the clear, vastness of it. Trees formed a protective barrier around his house. "Oh, this is pretty."

A small A-frame house was tucked in the corner, the log cabin exterior matching his house. It seemed to blend in with the nature around it so you didn't notice it, unless you were carefully studying every inch of his world.

He braced his hands on the pine railing on either side of her, his body heat welcome against her back. The nerves that had been eating her alive faded away, as if they had nothing against the sheer dominating power that was Doyle Kole. They had been quiet on the ferry ride over, taking her car because his stayed on the mainland so he had something to drive. It was currently parked at the loft.

Never in her wildest dreams would she think that this was where he lived, and yet looking at it now, she realized this was him. Strong lines, everything open.

"Let me show you my home." He took her hand and led the way inside. A round table with four chairs was in the small nook where she had exited. The kitchen was massive. An abandoned coffee mug sat on the island. Everything was wood, giving his house a warmth to it that was absent in both the penthouse and Jace's house. This, she realized, was a home. There was a difference.

He took her upstairs, the dark cherry-colored hardwood floor cool beneath her socks. Again, it was open from the main floor and up so you could stand anywhere on the stairs and see into the living room. Pictures decorated the wall. Pictures of Doyle with the girls, school pictures, one of the girls playing the guitar while another played with a dog, baby pictures, even a picture of his ex-wife in a wedding dress as another man kissed her. "You have a picture of her marrying someone else?"

"Yes."

"Why?"

"They're family." The simple statement made something sad and wistful slide through her. "This is Willy's room." He pushed the door open and she saw an unmade bed and clothes on the floor. Posters of favorite bands and some cute teen boys were on walls printed a vibrant turquoise color. "Dani's." It was at the other end of the short hall and she found herself staring into a bedroom of her childhood fantasies. It didn't have the fairy tale images, but the double bed had a canopy where Christmas lights draped under sheer blue fabric and coiled around the frame. It was a little messier. "I won't even let you see the girls' bathroom." He rapped his knuckles on a closed door. "They used it this morning so it'll be a fright. Closed doors are a rule here. No intruding. With two pre-teen girls, privacy is almost a requirement."

The low wall at the top of the stairs ended and he pushed open a closed door. "This is mine."

The walls were a dark grey color that somehow managed to not look institutional. A large king bed dominated one wall and the one across from it was all glass. On the other side was a balcony that looked like it matched the one downstairs. "You have a thing for windows."

"I can spend up to a year on a bus where there's nothing to look at but three other assholes. My bed is a bunk with no windows and light is pretty sparse. I'm a big guy. A bunk sucks ass. When I'm not there or in a hotel, I want to be surrounded by nothing but space."

Made sense. She wandered around, looking at his bedroom. A sensual painting of a woman in shadows made her pause. It wasn't the overt sexuality to it, it was the name Evers slashed boldly over the bottom right corner. "That's a Jensen Evers."

"Mm." He stretched out over the foot of his bed, his feet braced on the floor while he rose up on his elbows. He looked casual and sexual, relaxed yet not, as he watched her.

She turned back to the painting and the more she looked at it, the more she caught the subtle nuances of submission hidden in dark, smoky shadows. Only her lower leg was lit from the knee down. Her toe was pointed, a delicate chain on her ankle could've been jewelry but for the fact that the end of the chain disappeared into the darkness. One hand rested on her opposite hip, her arm blocking the view of her sex while her other arm was bent so nothing of her breasts were revealed. Her fingers touched her neck that arched in the dim light, her head disappearing into the dark but she could imagine a hand holding the hair, tilting her head back so her dom, could Kate see her face. Sexual, erotic, sensual and yet if you didn't know what you were looking at, you wouldn't see it for what it was: an erotic painting of submission. It made the back of her neck feel hot and her stomach feel tight. Her own sex had an aching fullness. Carefully clearing her throat, she went onto the next painting. Another Jensen Evers, this time it was a mermaid in a turquoise ocean. Seaweed coiled through her hair as it floated on invisible drafts. An octopus' tentacles were wrapped menacingly around her arms, arching her back in a graceful blow but for her hands which curled around the dark bonds.

The skin on her wrists tingled and Kate fluffed the front of her shirt because it was really warm in there. The other painting was a combination of oil and charcoal. A forest nymph entangled in vines, holding her to a tree. Like a submissive bound to a cross. She remembered what he said that first night about how he liked seeing a submissive on a cross. Holding the neck of her shirt against her mouth, she gazed at the painting.

"Open your jeans, Katey."

Her eyes closed at his voice, the tone of command sliding through her. Lowering her shaking hands, she opened her jeans as she gazed at the shadow smudges on the nymphs body. Not shadows, not dirt. Marks from a cane against willing skin. It would've come from the tree. She wanted to be that nymph with an aching intensity, to feel the cool vines on her skin as they held her against the tree, the rough bark on her bare skin while she waited for him to deliver another strike to her body.

"Are you wet?"

"Yes."

"Show me."

Oh Lord. Wetting her lips, she slid her hand down her stomach where a different kind of nerve fluttered away. Her breathing grew louder in his room as her fingers dipped beneath her panties and over the slick, aching folds of her sex. A knot on her bracelet rolled over her clit, making her gasp audibly. Her fingers were trembling when she lifted them up, her skin glistening with arousal.

"I have damage control to do, broken ground to heal, so I'm asking, do you consent, Katey?"

She nodded.

"Use your words, girl."

"Yes."

"Put your back to the wall so I can see you."

So she could see him. She did as he ordered. He was still sprawled on his bed, his upper body canted up by his bent arms. Looking at him made her heart beat faster.

"Nothing like a pretty sub with her hand down her

pants. Make yourself come."

The words were so different than what he usually told her to do, which was hold back and not orgasm. Having those dark eyes watching her was intimidating. His gaze scanned her from head to toe in a slow way that made her feel like every inch of her had just been studied. He rolled off the bed in a graceful movement and crossed to where she leaned against the wall.

Doyle braced his hand on the wall above her head. Reaching down, he drew her hand out and kissed her fingers. "You're not ready for this, are you?"

What did that mean? Of course she was.

"There's hesitation and uncertainty in your eyes. I broke something. Come on." Maintaining the hold on her hand, he led the way into the spacious bathroom and filled the tub that was before a floor-to-ceiling window. He left her sitting on the tub, the rumble and rush of water filling the silence. Glancing down at her bracelet, she fiddled with the closest knot. Was she hesitating with him? Turning her attention to the window, she took in the breathtaking view of the Strait of Georgia. She was in Doyle Kole's house on Galiano Island. Not the penthouse where he crashed and took random girls from Edge, but in his home. This was his sanctuary. She knew that. You didn't live on an island, even if it had other residents, if you weren't looking to get away from everything else. The door clicked shut and he came in and squirted some bubble bath into the running water.

He set the red container on the tub's edge and came over to her. She was drawn to her feet and he pushed her jeans and panties down. In the same economical way, he stripped her naked, then he picked her up, setting her in the tub. The sweet scent of artificial strawberries came to her and she reached for the container while bubbles grew around her. He had swiped it from his daughters if she went by the cartoon character on the front.

"Sit back," he said as he pressed his fingertips to her chest, nudging her back. Heated water wrapped around her while he sat on the floor, his legs stretched out and crossed at the ankles. He dipped his fingers in the water and adjusted the temperature a bit, watching her as the tub continued to fill.

"Why am I here?"

"Here?" He rapped his knuckles against the side of the tub, then drew a circle around them both. "Or here?"

"Both."

Doyle turned off the water, settling back against the wall. "Because you're unsure of me but not to the point where you won't be naked before me. Nice, by the way. There are no worries in the bath."

"I'm not unsure," she said as she scooped up a handful of bubbles, avoiding his intense stare that said he knew she was full of bullshit. She sighed as she made a fist, squishing the small frothy mountain. She had promised both him and herself that she'd be honest in this. She still wasn't sure exactly what this was, but if she was here after this morning, that had to mean something. Right? "Okay, maybe I am."

"Maybe you are. This morning you looked me dead in the eye and said red. I told you I'd always listen when you said stop. Do you want this to end? I can help you find a dom who is less of an asshole. It will piss me off, but I'll do it."

That made her look at him. At him, just not at the

large body sitting on the floor, watching her. "Why would it piss you off?"

He rested his forearm on the tub, his fist tapping out a slow and steady rhythm. In the space between his knuckles the word BEAT was inked. For the first time, she wondered if it was for more than the drums, a secret little homage to kink. The knuckles on his right hand had tiny images of different drums. In one magazine she had read, he had once joked that they were his gangsta tattoos and were therefore his most innocuous ones. "I could spout a lot of bullshit, but the simple fact is that I'm a possessive bastard and I guard what is mine like Scrooge."

In her chest, her heart made one hard knock in response before it began to race. "But you walked away from Claire." His fist stopped its tapping and his thumb began to quietly drum on the tub.

"Yes."

"I'm yours?"

His hand stilled completely. "Yes." The force of his stare made her shift in the bath, the water lapping against the sides. She slid to the foot of the tub, putting them closer so she could look into his eyes.

"You think I'm yours."

He leaned forward until only the wall of the tub was between them. "I *know* you're mine."

The bathroom that was as big as her bedroom shrank to the space of the tub. He ran his thumb over her lip; the back of his ring was warm from his skin. Reaching up, she caught his hand, lowering it so she could study his ring. "How did you know I did this?"

"Don't move." He left her in the tub but was back

shortly. She watched as he stripped. The man needed to be naked all the time because he was a thing of beauty. His arms covered from fingers to shoulders in dark images so that barely any skin showed, hard muscles that her fingers ached to memorize and the unabashed jutting of his aroused cock made everything melt in her. He stepped into the tub and sat down on the side so she was between his spread legs. The sun that shone through the window kissed his skin as if even Mother Nature knew he was a thing of beauty that needed to glow. "Turn around."

When she did, he drew her up so she had to shift to her knees. The press of his erection was like a hot brand between her shoulders and her nipples tightened at the sensation.

"Nice." He wiped his hand over her left breast, teasing the swollen tip until an ache slid through her body and settled between her legs. "Take care of this." He eased his ring off and she shook bubbles off her hand to hold it. Fingers combed through her hair and fisted hard, yanking her head back and dragging a surprised gasp from her. His face blurred briefly while a tension moved through her even as she felt her muscles melt away. "Open." When she parted her lips, he tucked the cap of a marker between her teeth. "Don't crack that. Why don't you put that free hand between those pretty legs and ease the ache."

No, Sir, and yes, Sir, please, she thought as he bent over her. The tip of the marker moved over her breast. A dampness that was warmer than the water greeted her fingers. The water shifted like an extra caress over swollen flesh.

"Don't drop my ring."

"No, Sir," she mumbled around the cap. Her body jerked as he wrote over her nipple and her fingers teased her throbbing clit.

"Don't make me fuck this up. Settle."

Slippery fingers ventured over and around her clit and when she shifted, her knees slid on the slick tub.

"Settle, Katey."

Being still was hard to do with him doing whatever to her breast, his stomach resting against her head and the presence of an erection that would not be ignored. When she stopped touching herself, he pinched her hard beneath her breast. "I didn't tell you to stop. Work that clit." The felt tip disappeared and he removed the cap from her mouth. He spun her around and with his hand still fisted in her hair, he guided her down so the thick head of his cock brushed over her lips. "Until you come, Katey girl. Don't drop my ring."

His hot skin was taut over the hardness and the salty pre-cum was almost cool against her tongue. Clutching his ring, she hooked her fist over the side of the tub, needing something to ground her. He maintained control, manipulating the speed in which she took him and the depth. When the teasing touches on her clit were no longer enough, she slid a finger in and he muffled her cry. He drew her off, guiding her up. Doyle's mouth slanted over hers, kissing her as her orgasm broke. Doyle caught her under her arms and lifted her so she was on his lap, water dripping to the floor.

"Do you still have my ring?"

Nodding without really tracking, she opened her fist. He plucked it up and held it between his thumb and index finger, the black wood on the left side. With the curve of the ring it made the letter D. "Doyle." He rolled it one hundred and eighty degrees. Sun shone through the two angled lines. "Kole." He shifted the ring right side up. Two thin lines were gently etched into the wood from the tip. "Mann."

He ran a finger over her breast. She looked down to see what he had drawn. There was a large autograph on her breast. Of a sorts. It was an upside down D with two lines angling out from the center for the K and to make it look like devil horns, two small lines came down from halfway between the lines. Doyle Kole. Unless you knew just a bit more in that in his birth name was Kolemann.

"That doesn't explain how you…"

He flipped the ring around and there as gently etched into the ebony as the fine lines in the ring was KJ. How had he even noticed it? It was so tiny she had to use two magnifying glasses to engrave her mark. She had practiced it for days. She had left off the note because it simply hadn't fit at that size. "Katey Jay. Now tell me you're not mine."

He slid his ring back on.

"How did you spot that?"

"I'm observant. What amazes me is that it's a perfect fit."

She ran her own thumb over the ring. "I'm observant," she said as she ran her thumbnail in one groove.

"You're talented. You on the pill?"

She nodded. Before she could process the question, he grabbed her hips and slid her forward. Clutching the back of his neck, she looked into his eyes as he eased into her. His eyes were so dark there was only a slight variation between his pupils and the iris. This close, she could see the inky black of his pupils dilate while his nostrils flared. "Oh yeah, you're fucking mine." He fisted his hand in her hair and kissed her as he took them both into the tub while he moved inside her.

Wrapping her legs around his hips, she rose up and sank down, feeling every inch of him inside her. "You said bare was a hard no."

"I want me inside and outside you." He cupped the breast he had autographed. Doyle brought her mouth to his again, kissing her deeply as he moved inside her. "Mine. You're mine, Katey."

Finally, she thought as his other hand gripped her ass, guiding her over him. *Finally she was someone's.*

With her feet tucked onto the seat of the chair under the blanket Doyle had tucked around her earlier, she watched him with his daughters. Apparently gathering around the fire pit was a common thing, even if it was a school night. The girls had given her cautious looks and she couldn't blame them. She had seen way too many women revolve through Jace's doors.

Doyle sat in the chair beside her and a guitar was balanced against him while he and Willow played and sang. His eldest had an amazing voice. It was crisp and clear with a touch of sweetness and a dash of smoke. Danielle was perched on the arm of his chair, leaning into him. Even though she wasn't playing or singing, she seemed a part of the moment.

Witnessing it made the back of Kate's eyes burn while her throat kept shrinking until it hurt to breathe.

He so clearly adored his daughters, his love wrapped around them. Envy squeezed her heart until she feared it would be pulverized.

Did they have any idea how lucky they were? To not just know they were loved but to feel safe in it? They were a part of his life. An important part. She felt like her nose was pressed up against an icy window that fogged with every exhale. Even his ex-wife and Oz were a part of his life. This was a family.

Seeing it, sitting among them, made her feel like that moment in the trailer when Jace and Carl had come in and she had hidden, too afraid to make her presence known. So afraid of the unknown and wanting what was beyond her hidden panel so badly she could taste it in her mouth.

Doyle reached up and ruffled Danielle's hair without seeming to miss a beat and Kate had to look away. All she had ever wanted was to feel that safe, that cherished. She pressed her nose into the blanket that smelled of wood smoke, pine and salt. Staring at the flames that licked over logs and sparked into the night sky, Kate tried really hard not to cry. Her cheeks hurt and her jaw ached from all that was boiling up inside. Her eyes closed as the voices of father and daughter in song wrapped around her, rubbing at old wounds she feared would never heal.

She was jealous of two little girls.

It was ridiculous, but true. She had never had this, never experienced it despite wanting it so bad. Now here she was, neck deep in it and yet again it wasn't for her. *Don't cry, don't cry.* She breathed through her mouth into the blanket, afraid if it was through her nose she'd sniffle.

Oh God, she could feel herself splintering apart, millions of cracks snapping open inside her as that broken down girl inside her began to hemorrhage.

"Okay, girls," Claire said, interrupting them, "wrap it up."

"But Mom." Kate didn't know which of the girls spoke, but it probably didn't matter.

"It's nine o'clock. There's no buts at nine pm."

"Fine." The music cut off in a discordant twist of notes as a hand slapped down on the strings.

"Willow." Doyle's voice said a lot. The tone was what Kate thought of as his dom voice. It meant no more bullshit, he expected utter obedience and he got it. Even from his daughter.

"Sorry." The almost teenager stomped off to the house. Doyle, Claire and Danielle followed.

They looked like a family. Even though there was a fracture between Doyle and Claire they were still very much a family. His daughters would never doubt that, never doubt him. He would, Kate knew, burn the world down to protect them. Watching them hurt. Muscles protested as she stretched out her legs and stood up.

"Are you okay?"

She had forgotten the other dom. Nodding, she pulled the blanket around her. "I—" She actually couldn't think of a single thing to say without her voice cracking. So instead, she turned and headed to the trees. Subtle lights glowed on the ground, solar lights Doyle had explained, though everyone knew the way back and forth. Put in years ago and pretty much forgotten.

Once she emerged on Doyle's side, she came to a stop and stared at the shadow of her car. She didn't know the hours of the ferry and she didn't really care. She went in his home that smelled of him and grabbed her keys.

Kate - 2014

With her forearms braced on her thighs, Kate studied the pale cream carpet and wondered, as she did every time, how the carpet was kept so clean. She briefly fantasized about tiny carpet elves who scoured each and every stain out with some magic concoction.

"Kate? You can go in now."

Grabbing her backpack, Kate left the spotless flooring behind. Every time she approached the door, she felt a nervous flutter in her chest and a panicky burst in her stomach that made her want to turn around and leave. The door closed behind her and she shook the nerves out of her hands.

"Every time, Kate. I don't bite."

She smiled as she set her bag down and sat on the sofa. "I know."

"Not without consent. Relax."

The comment was designed to make her laugh. Tucking her hands between her knees, she looked at Heather Davis who gave her a kind smile as she sipped her coffee. She had been coming to Heather for a year now; and yet again, she was thankful for having found her.

"How was it?"

Kate entwined her fingers and exhaled slowly. "Terrifying. Overwhelming. Amazing." Her last word made Heather sit back in her chair, setting her mug down on the glass table.

Walking into Edge had been one of the scariest things she had ever done. The club was designed to intimidate, reminding her of gladiator movies where the show was in the arena. It even looked like one with its circular levels only decorated in dark woods and dark leather. The lowest level had taken her breath away with all its various implements of pleasure and pain. They should have scared her and sent her scurrying back home.

Only nothing had until last night.

For that she could thank Heather. After she had a disastrous experience with a dom she had met online, Kate had decided she needed help. She had sought out someone to talk to. Her first counselor hadn't been a good fit. Heather had been the third one and Kate hadn't just found someone to talk to about her childhood with her mother, Jace, and even her rape, but someone who was also in the D/s world. For the first time in a long time she hadn't felt utterly alone with everything in her head. Talking helped because she no longer felt like she was drowning.

Heather studied her with a knowing eye. "Something happened."

Kate took in a shaky breath and began to fiddle with the knots on her bracelet. "I…" She shrugged because finding the words was hard. How did she explain what had happened? To look up and realize all of her worlds had collided at seeing familiar eyes watching her. "I saw someone I know at Edge."

Heather waited. It was one of the things Kate appreciated most about her. She knew when to push and when to wait. Kate figured it was the dominant within her. Kate watched her left thumb and middle finger twist and roll the knot around. "Do you remember when asked me about the moment when things woke up for me?"

"Things? Use your words, Kate."

Blushing, she cleared her throat. "Sex." One elegantly manicured nail tapped on the arm of Heather's chair and Kate took a calming breath. "My sexuality and sensuality." She was rewarded with a pleased smile and something eased within.

"Yes."

"He was there. He was at Edge." Kate peeked up and saw that she had finally, after three years, managed to surprise Heather. A slim eyebrow arched up.

"What did you do?"

"Ran, I ran."

"Why?"

Because, Kate thought as she sank back on the sofa, it was Doyle Kole. He still scared her, but not like he had when she had been a kid. He scared her because he made her want. "What if I'm not ready?"

"Only you can truly answer that, Kate. But I want you to think carefully before you answer. What brought you here?"

Fiddling with her bracelet, she looked away from her therapist. Want, she thought. Always wanting. Not just wanting to submit someone or being with someone, but wanting to reclaim all the pieces of herself. Pieces she had lost to her mother, to Jace, to the man who had hurt her and pieces she hadn't even known she had lost. Relaxing her hand, she let go of the bracelet and looked at Heather. The older woman gave her a gentle smile as she lifted her mug.

Chapter 14

"KATEY?" HIS HOUSE was dark and silent. Taking the stairs two at a time, Doyle raced to the second floor. After a brief talk with Willow about her contest entry and trying not to get into an argument with Claire, he had stepped out of his former house to find Kate gone and Oz looking concerned. He didn't know what had happened tonight, but something had. He gave his bedroom a quick look to see it was as empty as the rest of his house.

The open door on his deck made him jerk back into the room. She sat against the glass, looking out into the night, and relief pumped through him. Stepping out, he looked at her with the blanket wrapped snug around her. Walking over to her, he braced his feet on either side of her hips and sat down. He tugged the blanket closer around her and folded his arms on her knees.

"They're lucky girls," she said in a quiet voice.

"I'm the lucky one," he corrected. He wished he had turned a light on so he could see her. There was a reason why she was sitting out here in the dark though.

"I don't think they like me."

"They're not used to sharing me." Dani had actually

told him that Kate had the saddest eyes she had ever seen. His youngest was observant. "Give it time."

"You love them so much."

Fuck. Lowering his chin to his arms, he started to make out her features in the dark as his eyes adjusted. He nodded because his girls were his life.

"I knew the first time Jace saw me that he wanted nothing to do with me. He wanted me to stay in that crappy trailer with a junky mother who would do anything for her next score or let me get swallowed up in the foster system. He looked at me like Mom did. I stopped pretending really early."

"You're going to break my heart, aren't you?" He squeezed her knee and she shrugged. A tightness grew in his chest. They had all contributed to those shadows in her eyes. Jace because he was a selfish bastard, him and the others because not one of them had done a damn thing about it. No sane person should've given Jace custody of a child.

"I didn't even think I still believed in dreams until I stood in that lawyer's office, waiting to meet him. I didn't know if she had lied, picked someone famous and said that was my dad. It's hard to believe the stories an addict tells, but I wanted it. I wanted him to be my dad so bad. My life would change. Like Cinderella or Annie. Whisked off to the castle or mansion, and all the shit disappeared. It didn't. Not at all." Her voice broke and her head thumped against the window. She was more than breaking his heart, she was clawing at it.

"There was this space under the bench in the trailer. She used to make me go there whenever a john or dealer came over. Not to protect me, but because I got in the way. I wanted him to be my dad so bad and that he'd come and rescue me, I covered the entire inside of that box with pictures of him. Pictures I'd tear out of the magazines she would cry over. When I moved in with him, I still did it. Because I still wanted him to be that guy in my dreams. The one who saved me. Rescued me," she whispered.

Ah shit, he didn't want to hear this. He didn't want to see the pain bleeding from her because he couldn't fix this. He couldn't stop the scene and make it better. There was no safe word in this, no red.

"If Willow came to you and said someone scared her, what would you do?"

Fucking Jace-fucking-Jennings. "Depends. If it was a kid, scare him. If it wasn't, I'd end him."

"Like I said. Lucky girls. There's a box at the other end of the deck. I hate it. I hate everything inside it. What I hate most about it though is that he didn't care, Doyle. He didn't care about me at all." Her voice cracked and she covered her mouth and nose with her hands, her body shaking. "I hate him, I hate him so much." She hiccupped, the broken gasps tearing at him.

"I know, baby." He slid his hand behind her head and drew her close. She clutched the back of his shirt, her body jerking and shivering as she let it out. Her shaky breaths were hot against his neck while her face was cool. "Let's get you inside." He stood and scooped her up. He ignored the box, not ready to face whatever was in it, as he entered his room, drawing the door shut. He peeled off the blanket that smelled of smoke and heartache, palmed off her shoes then toed off his own. With both of them fully dressed, he eased them under the covers where he held her. A part of him wanted to offer her promises but he worried that she wouldn't believe them. What could he say?

She didn't cry. No tears slid over his skin as he held her through her pain. It was as if Jace-fucking-Jennings had broken her so completely there was nothing left. The trembling of her body gradually faded and the short, jerky breaths evened out and he knew she slept. Smoothing his hand down her hair, he continued to hold her because he needed to. He needed the contact with her. He hadn't brought her here to hurt her and yet he had unintentionally done that.

The thought made him ease out from beneath her. Doyle stripped Kate out of her jeans and left her sleeping in the bed. Walking out onto his balcony, he crouched by the box. That was a shit ton of tape to keep something from getting out. Picking the box up, he carried it down to the kitchen and stared at it. It wasn't a matter of not opening the box, the question was whether he wanted to do this with Kate or without. Deciding she was hurting enough for the evening, he opted to tackle the box on his own.

He grabbed a knife and tapped it on the island, a quick, staccato rhythm before he went hunting for the seams through the tape.

Nothing good was inside. Once the flaps were freed, Doyle braced his hands on the butcher block and found himself hesitating to look in. "Fuck this shit." He flipped the flaps open. The box was only half-full and he stared down at a hockey jersey. It was child size and would fit the girls. Pulling the shirt out, he turned it, expecting to see Jennings on the back. Instead the word No was above the number one. A pile of envelopes were bound together with a rubber band and when he went to peel it off, the elastic broke apart. Lifting the flap on the envelope, he eased out a piece of paper. *Happy birthday, pretty, little No. One* was printed in bold masculine printing. He slid the note back in and proceeded to go through every envelope. Halfway through the pile for everything began to click. Not short hand for number like he had thought but no as in no one, as in nobody. He stared hard at the jersey, then started from the beginning.

As a dom, he knew about the mind fuck. In his world it was a game, foreplay. This was a total mind fuck. Not a game but a hunt. This was warfare on a vulnerable girl. Some of the envelopes were still sealed and he happily slashed them open with the knife. "Fuck."

The photos were obscene and something no child should see. He was relieved she had stopped looking at this point. This would've broken her beyond anything. Carefully, he eased the graphic images of the man who had hurt her back into their envelopes. Bracing his hands on the island, Doyle bent over at the waist. "Fuck," he said, slamming his hands on the counter as he shouted his favorite word into the claustrophobic silence of his kitchen.

He wanted a drink. Needed one. Needed the alcohol to wash away what he had revealed. She had been a baby. The age of his girls. She had been utterly alone in this. Snatching up the cordless phone, he dialed.

"Doyle? What's–"

"Let me talk to Willy."

"What? No. It's three in the morning."

"Put her on the phone."

"Are you drunk?"

The typical question made him snarl. "Are you fuck-ing serious?"

"It's three in th–"

"What's wrong?" Oz had grabbed the phone from Claire.

"I need to talk to Willy and Dani. I'd come over, but if Kate wakes up, she'd be alone with all this shit and I can't leave her alone with all this shit. Put my daughter on the fucking phone, Oz."

"Okay. What's going on, D? This isn't like you."

Doyle stared at the jersey. "It's been a helluva fucking night."

"What happened with Kate? Hold on. Willow, hon-ey."

He could hear his daughter's sleepy response and the phone changed hands. "Dad?"

He thought of Kate telling him that Jace hadn't given a shit about her, asking him what he'd do. What would he do if someone had stalked his girls like this? What wouldn't he do?

He needed to know his girls were safe. That there was nothing like this happening to them. That in ten years he wouldn't find another box like this. "You know I love you, right?"

"I know. I love you too."

"You know you can come to me if someone was hurt-ing your or scaring you? No matter where I was in the world?"

His oldest was quiet. "Yes. Daddy, are you okay? You sound mad."

"I am but not at you. It's why I needed to hear your

voice. I love you, Willy."

"Love you back."

"Go back to sleep, baby. I'll see you tomorrow."

"Okay. Night."

"Night. Give the phone to Oz." He heard her say that she was worried about him and Oz said he'd take care of it.

He wanted to burn everything. Every envelope that called her no one. Every little letter that made her feel small and scared. He flipped the jersey over and stared at the logo. Pretty specific. Pretty fucking specific. Throw in the tickets to hockey games and it didn't take a genius to put the pieces together.

Oz woke up Dani and he had the same conversation with her, reassuring himself. "What happened, Doyle?" His friend's voice was low and had a hard edge to it that didn't come out very often. "Don't bullshit me. You're freaking out; you've worried the girls. What's going down?"

Instead of answering, Doyle hung up and tossed the phone aside.

What could he possible say? Dragging his hands through his hair, he fisted the strands as he glared at what had hurt her. Gathering everything up, he tossed them back in the box and put the collection of evil in the garage so the girls wouldn't get nosy. His fist slammed on the light switch, plunging the kitchen into darkness and he went up to Kate. That's where he needed to be.

Not downstairs gazing at a past he couldn't fix or change.

A smart man would probably hole up for a few days. Doyle wasn't feeling smart. He was feeling violent.

With one foot braced on the table, he slouched on the leather couch as he typed on his phone. Today the band was meeting at the penthouse to hash out the latest album. They were pretty much sequestered in the studio room. Probably not the wisest place for him to be: in an enclosed area with Jace-fucking-Jennings looking hung over. "Hey," without looking up from his phone, he spoke to the lead singer, "what was that douche bag hockey player's name?"

Opening a message window, he hesitated before he typed in Jasmine Lane's name. *What's the expiration date on sexual assault?* Unlike with Kate's box, he very much felt like he was trespassing. Jasmine wasn't just a domme at Edge, she was a lawyer. He and Kate hadn't mentioned the contents of the box after she had pointed it out. This morning she had dropped him off at the penthouse while she had gone to class as if nothing monumental had happened.

JASMINE: What?! How are the girls? I'm phoning you. Right. Now.

DOYLE: *In studio. Girls are fine, more than. Think hypothetical.* He closed the conversation and turned off the ringer.

"Hockey dou…ooooh Berger." A chortle came from Jace and Doyle glanced up before turning his attention to the phone. "Funny guy."

His thumbs moved over the screen keyboard as he texted Kate. *FYI I'm going to beat the fuck out of Jace.* His screen lit up with Jasmine's call as it vibrated in his hands. He hit ignore call because he wasn't about to discuss this with someone who had the ability to fix things without talking to Kate. He just needed to do something.

Even if it was smashing his fist into Jace's face.

"Berger?" He asked as carefully as he could. The name didn't twig his memory but he wasn't exactly buddy buddy with all of Jace's douche friends.

"Josef Henzberger."

"Ketchup," Max muttered as he glared, tuning his guitar. "Who fucked with this?"

His phone gave a shudder to tell him he had a voicemail and a text. He opened up the conversation with Kate. *Don't hurt your hand.*

Her response was so surprising, a grunt of amusement escaped. Funny girl. His screen lit up with a text from Jasmine. *God damn it, answer your phone!*

In studio. Answer. He switched to the browser and put in the asshole's name.

"Berger was a machine," Jace said. "Always scored amazing pussy."

Doyle went still. As those words pinged around his brain, seeing Kate crying on his deck played back. He didn't remember moving but suddenly he was using the massive coffee table as a stepping stone. Without hesitating, both of his hands fisted on the front of Jace's shirt and he dragged him over the back of the chair. Surprised shouts came from the guys, but he didn't care as he slammed the singer into the wall with enough force to make the man grunt.

An arm hooked around his neck as someone tried to peel him off while they shouted in his ear to let Jace go.

"Did you know, you piece of shit?" Doyle eased Jace forward then slammed him hard into the wall again. "Did you know?" The words were shouted in Jace's face as he ignored the frantic tugs. "You heartless motherfucker, did you know what he was doing? Stalking her like prey, breaking her down. Stop touching me," he snarled at whomever was on his back, tugging frantically. "When she came to you scared and terrified, needing you to step up, did you just shrug her off? She is your fucking daughter!" He slammed Jace into the wall again. "Did you know? Answer me!"

"Fuck, D. What is your–"

He pressed his forearm over Jace's throat, cutting off his air and words. "You think carefully, you son of a bitch, about what is going to come out of your mouth."

"Jesus, D, you're going to choke him. Knock it off."

"You left her alone. She was a kid. *Your* kid. Bad enough you left her with Beli, but did you leave her with that molesting motherfucker?" The grip on him went slack and a heavy silence hit the room. "She came to you. Even knowing you wouldn't do a god damn thing, she came to you. I've forgiven you for a lot of your bullshit, asshole, including fucking my wife, but I cannot forgive you for Kate. You broke her. You broke her heart, you broke her childhood. I want to kill you for that." He eased his arm off and Jace gasped for breath, his face red, sweat sliding down his temple, while his pulse jumped and pounded in his neck. "I could kill you for that, but I'll be fucking damned if I leave her alone because my ass winds up in jail. You did this to her, Jace, just as much as your buddy Berger." He pushed his face close so he could smell the man's fear. Jace's head pushed back as if to get away from him.

"Jesus, D. What the fuck?"

Doyle ignored Max's whispered words as he stared at Jace. The eyes the same color as his daughter's shifted away. This man…this asshole who had hurt his Katey. Left her alone with her junky mother and a molester. He grabbed the other man's jaw and made Jace look at him. "He stalked her in your house. Had access to her room in your house. He terrorized her in your house. He raped her in your house. And you, you fucker, sit here and have the balls to say the man is a pussy god? She is your daughter and you just gave her to him. You, Jace. This is on you. Fuck you. I'm done." He pushed Jace's head into the wall because there was all this rage in him about thinking of Kate in that room, that box of shit in his garage. Doyle slammed his fist in the mouth that had made them all wealthy. He felt a tooth cut into a knuckle as blood splattered. He let Jace fall to the floor, bleeding and still trying to get his breath back.

Calmly, Doyle walked over to where his phone had been dropped and with the others looking from him to Jace then at each other in an awkward silence, he walked out.

He didn't look back.

"You're fucking him."

The statement was as unexpected as the voice. Looking up from the collection of sketches and photos spread over her bed of her final school project, which centered around the violin necklace, Kate stared blankly at the man standing in her doorway. If asked out of all the people she knew, who she least expected to show up at her small, over-crowded apartment, Jace wouldn't even be on the shortlist.

There was faint bruising under his eyes and his lip

was swollen from Doyle's fist. Eyes like hers glared at her.

It wasn't a question, so she didn't answer. Mostly because shock had robbed her of her voice. Shock because he knew where she lived.

He stood before her as if he had any right to judge her. She loved him. The little girl inside her would always love him, would always crave his love and approval, even though, as an adult, she knew that was never going to happen. She also hated him. With the same intensity of that scared and needy little girl, she hated him. For constantly letting her down and for breaking her heart.

He would never win father of the year, would never even be nominated. So by what right did he have to come into her home, such that it was, and say anything to her?

Kate let all her thoughts swirl around and settle as she looked at Jace. In the ten years she had lived in his home, he had changed. A lifetime of drinking and drugs was starting to take their toll and the good looks that had been there in his thirties were starting to look brittle, making him appear older than he was. Time and life were making their presence known. She knew that she would always see that golden bad boy Mom had loved so much, that face in the photos that had lined the walls of her safe spots. Not that he had never done anything to make her feel safe. Jace Jennings was a mirage. A shimmery image in the distance that a lonely and scared child clung to, and when she got closer, Kate realized there was nothing there.

"How old am I?" Her question made him blink. "When's my birthday? What's my middle name?" He simply stood there.

"What does that matter? You're fucking Doyle and I

want you to stop before you ruin everything even more."

The words hurt in a way that they shouldn't. That's how he saw her? As something that had ruined his life. Well, he had ruined hers too. "It matters a lot and your answers will determine the outcome of this conversation." They were having a conversation. Probably their first one ever. He glared at her, like a sulky teenager who was giving the silent treatment because he didn't have the answers.

"I'm twenty-four. January third. My middle name is Jace. The last name on my birth certificate is Jennings, for the record. That was the name she gave me: Kate Jace Jennings. You know nothing about me." She looked down at her sketches, embracing the hurt that statement left her with. She heard Doyle's voice in her head, telling her to take it in, hold it, because that's what he made her do when something hurt or felt really good. Take the hurt, feel it, learn it.

Now let it go.

Lifting her lashes, she looked at her father. She never called him that. She would never call him that. He was and always would be Jace. He was just a guy, one wearing bruises Doyle had put on him. Because of her, because Jace had failed her. Jace had hurt her. Just a guy. "You don't get to tell me what to do. You don't get to storm into my home and tell me who I can or cannot be involved with because he got tired of your bullshit. That's all you are — bullshit." She sat up a little straighter, feeling like something heavy just fell off her back. "Do you really think if I'm not involved with Doyle he'll come back? That he'll forgive you for being a shitty co-worker and even less of a friend? You slept with his wife. Not because you loved her or even because you liked her. You fucked her because you could. You didn't want me. You never wanted me. I bet it was Charles who said you had to step up after the social worker contacted you, because it was like that Christmas spread right? Good PR. Legally you're my father. Genetically you're my father. But that's it. You're not my dad so you don't get to come in here and suddenly tell me what to do. I'm twenty-four, that makes me an adult, and I can fuck whomever I want. This isn't even about me and Doyle. This is about you. That's the problem. It's always been about you."

Kate's heart felt like it was being squeezed as she looked at Jace. Damn, but she wanted him to still be a dad to her. To just once be the father of her childhood dreams.

Take the hurt, hold it. Let it go.

"But it's not. It should also be about me." She flattened her hand over the spot that hurt, that felt tight and empty. It would always feel tight and hollow because that's the spot that he should've been in, he should've filled. It was a small spot though. She could live with a tiny, hollow piece because those bruises on his face let her know she wasn't alone. He wasn't everything. She didn't need him.

Just his name. She already had that. She let go.

"You need to go." Dismissing him, she turned her attention back down to her bed, to her dream. It wasn't even a dream, was it? A dream was something intangible. The shimmery image in the distance. Only when she was close, this was real. Not like the oasis that was Jace. This wasn't the pot at the end of the rainbow. This *was* the rainbow.

She heard his voice in the hallway but she didn't listen. Probably talking to one of her roommates that he was going to go fuck, because that's what he did. Grasped at whoever loved him for a moment, because that was easier than Kate. Being wanted he could handle, being needed he couldn't. And...

She didn't need him anymore.

Her vision blurred for a minute as that realization hit.

Not because she needed Doyle. She didn't need him either, because she had Kate.

"Huh," she said softly in the solitude of her bedroom. Reaching for her cell, she sent a quick text to Doyle: *I may or may not have told Jace off.*

A soft chime followed and she looked up with the same sense of surprise as when she had found Jace standing there. Unlike that moment, he was utterly welcome. She smiled as Doyle leaned one tattooed shoulder against the doorframe, the relaxed pose of a bad ass. He typed onto his phone and the response showed up on hers. *You did.*

"So, I don't get to hit him again?"

Kate grinned at his question because he looked like he wanted to take another swing at Jace. "You can if you want, but no, you don't need to hit him again."

"Pity. It was rather enjoyable." He pushed off and walked into her room, shutting the door. "If those papers are important, you need to move them."

"Oh?"

"Mmm. Would hate to destroy them when I ravish you."

Her eyebrows rose even as she began to gather everything up. "I'm going to be ravished?"

He smirked as he grabbed the back of his shirt and dragged it over his head. Kate sat on her bed and took in the sheer perfection that was Doyle without a shirt. "The real question is, when aren't you being ravished?"

He had a valid point.

"Look at you," he said as he put a knee on her mattress and captured her face between his hands, tilting it up, "finding your voice. Amazing. I came here wanting to show you something and instead I was shown something. Amazing," he repeated before he commenced with the ravishing.

Chapter 15

RESTING HER CHEEK on her bent knees, Kate watched the dancing flames in the fireplace. There was something comforting about the warmth that radiated out mixed with the scent of burning wood. She liked Doyle's house. She liked the simplicity of it, the hominess of it. The steady thump of feet on the stairs had her watching Doyle. World War Tween had erupted between the sisters over sink space and not even Doyle's shouts up at them had broken up the fight. After he had gone up, Willow had stormed down, slamming the door to the half bath after stopping on the stairs to shout at both her father and sister. Doyle had simply stood at the top of the stairs, staring at his oldest, who had finally screamed "Fine!" before the door slamming.

It had been an interesting look for Kate into the life of a healthy family. Never would she have shouted at Jace as a teen and her relationship with her own sister was non-existent. She actually found herself wishing there was something between her and Natalie. To have her sister tantrum at her like that. There was too much poison in their pond though. Shaelynn hated Kate. Hated her. She hated Jace too, but he was the money. Kate was an easy target so Shaelynn had poured all that bad energy into polluting any kind of relationship between Jace's daughters.

So to watch the two sisters fight and scream while doors were slammed had been a peek into a window that was forever boarded up to her.

Doyle flopped onto the couch, dragging his hands down his face. "They're like gremlins. All cute and furry until the double digits hit before then they mutate into volatile little things I want to zap in the microwave." He made an exploding noise while popping out his fingers like bombs going off. "Puberty is awesome." He sighed.

"This is just the beginning."

He glared at her and Kate grinned in response. He reached out, grabbed under her legs and yanked so her feet rested on his lap. In a graceful move, he rolled so he lay on top of her, his arms folded over her thighs and his chin resting on his stacked hands. "Dani showed me her bracelet."

While Doyle and Willow had been working on Willow's song, Kate had been sitting on the lower deck listening while she looked in the toolbox she used for school, determined to make something out of the pieces from the neck of a violin. What was supposed to be a bracelet had turned into a pile of wooden pieces that wanted to go back to being a violin. She had enlisted the help of Danielle, who had been feeling a little left out. They hadn't come up with a solution to the jewelry puzzle, but Kate had ended up making a simple bracelet with guitar strings, a couple slices of the ebony fingerboard and some alphabet beads that were in her toolbox. She had put the letters in a mishmash order but when they were spaced out along the metal strings they spelled out dream. It was so cute she was going to make an entire line for the store.

"You do know Dani's jewelry is what started the battle."

"Oh?"

"Dani flaunted. Willy responded. It moved to a territorial war over the sink and you know the rest."

"I guess Willy needs one too."

He nodded. "She is the only one in the house without a Katey Jay design."

That explained the stink eye she was given when Willow stormed into the bathroom. "Can't have that."

"No. Don't move." He rolled off her and disappeared into the kitchen.

Reaching back to adjust the pillow, she scooted down so she was on her side, watching the fire dance and pop. The relaxed feeling evaporated when he set a box on the coffee table. A familiar box.

Her stomach snapped tight and she sat up where he had been before, putting as much space between her and the box. He sat on the table and braced his elbows on his knees, watching her watch the box.

She had briefly wondered where it had gone, but she hadn't let herself think about it anymore, pushing the contents presence back and back and back. "You opened it." She saw the sliced edges and the tucked ends of the flaps that kept the box shut.

He nodded.

"Why? Why would you…why?"

"Because it pains you." Her gaze skittered to him and his midnight stare was steady on her. She nervously tucked her hair behind her ear and tried to not look at the box. "You wanted me to or else you wouldn't have brought it here. Right?"

She shrugged one shoulder, not particularly wanting to talk about this. Her nervous fingers dropped down to her bracelet where she began to worry the hell out of the first knot she found. He reached out and covered her hand with his, stopping the fidgeting.

"Look at me, Kate."

She did, not realizing she was back to watching the box as if expecting it to come alive and devour her whole. His thumb stroked over the thin leather cords, brushing her skin; his touch calming.

"Nothing," Doyle said in a tone that demanded she listen, "in that box will hurt you again."

"Yes, it will."

He shook his head and she hissed when he pressed on one of the knots, making her look at him. "Only ghosts are in that box. Past hurts that left scars but cannot leave fresh wounds. You have carried the ghosts, and now I'll carry the load. Is that not why you brought it here?"

She nodded, watching his thumb gently rub over where he had caused the small hurt. "Okay," he said as he pushed her along the couch and turned her so her back was to the box of memories. He shifted onto the couch and pulled her forward, draping her legs over his thighs. "What do you want to do with it now?"

"I don't know." What she wanted for it never have existed in the first place. Resting her head against chest, she felt exhausted. Doyle rested his chin on her head, waiting. "Burn it?"

"You haven't kept all that shit for this long to set it on fire." One hand rubbed soothing circles on the small of her back while the other rested on her thigh. She hated logic. It was so damn logical. She sighed heavily, shrugging a shoulder. His voice became low and gentle as he spoke. "What would you say if I told you that within the province of British Columbia, there is no statute of limitations on sexual abuse?"

Her breath lodged in her chest and she drew her legs back, wrapping her arms around him as she looked up at him through her lashes. "I would ask why the drummer of a rock band would know that information."

One tattooed arm stretched over the back of the couch, his thumb beating a slow rhythm that made the small inked demon nod at her. "I asked a lawyer friend of mine."

"You talked to someone about me?"

"No. I asked a question and she's now panicking at the thought that one of the girls has been molested. So that's fun. Before you get defensive and pissed and offended, as the women in my life tend to get, I want you to ask yourself one important question, Katey Jay. Why did you save everything?" He leaned forward, rested his arm on her bent knees and put his face close to hers.

"I don't throw anything away." Lame, she thought as those dark eyes looked at her and through the weak answer. That was really…lame.

"Bull shit. Why have you kept everything if you didn't want someone to see, someone to know…someone to believe? Now I'm putting that shit away again because I'll be fucking damned if you start going through it, hurting yourself when you don't need to, and because the very knowledge of its existence makes me want to hunt that fucker down and beat him down." Despite the violent threat, he pressed a sweet kiss to her forehead and left her sitting there with the conversation spinning around her brain.

Her forehead fell against her knees. "Red," she whispered because she couldn't do this. Whatever he was implying, she didn't know if she wanted to face not just a lawyer but *him*. She also wasn't sure if the him in her head was Jace or his friend.

Red, she thought with a panicky desperation. *Red.*

She told herself it wasn't sneaking away when she had to wait until morning to catch the first ferry. She wasn't running away, she was going to work in her studio to finish the violin concerto piece and then work on her pieces for her courses.

Sitting on her stool at her work table, she stared blankly at her sketches without seeing the drawings. Shaking her head, she made herself focus. The concerto piece was by far the more complex so she reached for that one. She lost herself in the precise placement of the black gems as she duplicated the music. Her fingers found the familiar rhythm she had developed so the notes would be visible whether the piece was being worn or laid out. Time melted away as did thoughts of Doyle and lawyers and *him*. There was just the necklace.

Finally there was no more necklace to create.

She had known she was close to finishing it but to suddenly have the piece done left her feeling a little lost. With her hands resting on her lap, she stared from the necklace then back up to the music. Was it playable?

What if it wasn't?

Fuck. What if it *was*?

Her fingers hurt from working for—she paused and looked at her phone and saw she had missed quite a few texts from Doyle—almost five hours. Her stomach rumbled and her back was sore from hunching over. Even her ass was sore from sitting. She had paused briefly for a bathroom break, shifting from sitting to standing then sitting again until she had simply forgotten to move, as if sensing the finish line.

Grabbing her phone, she went into the kitchen, made herself a peanut butter sandwich and sat on the couch to eat while reading through Doyle's texts.

Am good, she reassured him, *was working. Sorry.*

Only that made her think of why she had fled.

Are you okay, Kate?

A Kate. Serious. He so rarely called her Kate. Only when he really wanted her attention. Was she okay? No. Yes. Maybe. She shrugged as she lay down on her back. That's what she told him before her sleepless night and constant working during the day grabbed her by the ankles and pulled her under.

Hands on her. Fear. Pain. *The pain.*

Her entire body jerked and she tried to remember where she was. Everything was familiar yet it felt wrong. Her workshop was shrinking closing in on her and she covered her eyes to make it stop. She swore she could still feel his hands on her, hear his "Hello, pretty little No One."

"Stop, stop, stop," she whispered. *Doyle.*

His name whispered through her and she began to pat around looking for her phone. Desperation clawed at her and she flipped over, searching for the lifeline. She found it on the floor. Her hands shook as she tried to remember the simple code to get into her phone. Finally she found the right numbers that opened it up and she found the right image to tap. Bending her legs, she pressed her forehead against her knees.

"Hello my Katey Jay."

His greeting wrapped around her, his deep voice so clear and warm she half expected to look up and see him. "Hi," she returned, her swirling thoughts settling. "I finished the violin piece."

It wasn't what she wanted to say. There was the nightmare that had clawed at her, the uncertainty that had developed at hearing the word lawyer in conjunction with *him*, but what had come out wasn't why she had called.

Why should all that shit rain on one important truth. She had finished her first contracted work. Exhaling softly, she looked to her workbench and smiled. "It's gorgeous. Doyle, it's so beautiful. *I* made it. Me!" His chuckle was low and the warm feeling grew. "Come see it?"

"Already on my way."

From the outside, Wallace's looked like a dive bar where you'd get shanked going in or out. The inside wasn't that much better. Appearances were deceiving. Wallace's was a bar where many Canadian bands, like Cyanide, had been discovered. If you wanted a music career, this was the place to come. The line up had curled around the corner of the building. If not for her name on a list, odds were she'd still be standing outside.

People were everywhere: standing, filling up the tables and crowding the dance floor.

A stage took up an entire wall and a band was rocking out a cover of a Soundgarden song and they weren't bad. The decor clung to the dive bar feeling, with neon signs on the walls and the dark, almost dingy walls and floor. People didn't come to Wallace's for shiny and trendy. They came for the music.

By the stage there was a booth and she recognized a couple of the guys sitting down. They were like her, kids of Cyanide, but unlike her they were following in their famous fathers' footsteps with their band Hysteria. She hadn't interacted with them in years. She wasn't here to see the opening band, Neon. Or even to see the second show with Hysteria. She was here for the unknown third act. She wondered if anyone knew what was coming.

There was something in the air, a crazy vibe of anticipation, and it seemed to add to the chaos.

It had been a hard week. In the shadows of the night, where memories crawled and clawed, she would open up her laptop, Google Josef Henzberger and be unable to sleep when she read an article, stared at his sports stats or saw a picture of him.

Not the smartest thing she had ever done. Sheer desperation had made her call her therapist.

To say dominant Doyle wasn't too happy with her was an understatement. They hadn't really talked about the lawyer, but it was always there. Swirling around her brain with horrible thoughts of what if. What if because she had been so scared he had done the same thing to other girls? Did that make it her fault? What if she had said something sooner? What if she did something now, what happened?

Even now, in this space that spoke to her of Doyle

and his passion for music, *he* was in the back of her head. Crowding and taunting her. Haunting and hurting her.

"Miss Jennings? This way please."

Turning at her name, she blinked at a bouncer. "Am I being bounced?"

He grinned. "Not yet. The night is young. Please." He led the way through the bar that began to scream in excitement since the band was done their set. They began to break down the stage, unplugging their equipment, and like a well-tuned machine, departed with a wave. The booth was empty, which meant Hysteria was backstage.She was led through a door marked stage, a second bouncer nodding.

She was not being thrown out.

Nerves began to prick at her fingers. There was a door marked private and one with office. The bouncer rapped knuckles against the office door then opened it for her.

Oh Lord.

Doyle leaned against the desk, his heavily inked arms folded over his chest bared by a leather vest. With the black jeans and biker boots he wore, he looked more like a bad-ass biker than the soon to be ex-drummer of a rock band.

"I'm not Jace, Katey."

"I know," she said fidgeting with her bracelet while he watched her, a man made up of bad attitude.

"Do you?" He looked down at her and she nodded. Reaching out, he snagged her fidgeting fingers and pulled her close, putting his lips against her ear. "I am not Jace," he repeated.

Through the door, she heard a man introduce Hysteria and the screams of the crowd followed were even louder than the previous wave. Their popularity took her by surprise. She couldn't look away from Doyle. "I know."

"So this adult version of you hiding under the bed isn't going to fly. You won't like the outcome next time you have the need to run and hide from me because I will take it to mean this is done. You don't like what I've done? You call me a bastard to my face and don't imply it."

"I wasn't." Her thumb flicked one of the knots rhythmically on her bracelet and he pressed a finger down, halting the nervous tell. "I wasn't. That's not why—" A sigh escaped and she leaned against him. "You complicate things," she admitted.

"Do you know what really complicates things? Grade seven math. That shit is crazy now. Me? I simplify things. Strip them down to the basics."

That made her snort.

"You doubt me? Watch." He lifted her left hand, ran his thumb over the bare skin. "I want you on your knees," he ordered, his low voice made her heart beat faster while the demand left her breathless. "Now."

He let go of her, and as if her knees melted away, she sank down on the floor of the office. The floor was cool against her bare legs. She wished she had worn something other than a snug denim skirt that ended above her knees. Fingers combed through her hair before suddenly fisting and pulling her head back so she was looking up at him. The way those black eyes watched her made her quiver and her panties grew damp in response. The force of his stare held memories of every time he took her over. In his eyes, she saw everything she had desired: not just a dom but one she trusted.

"Want me to make it even more simple?"

She nodded and took a shaky breath. "Yes, Sir." A light tug on her hair had her squeezing her thighs together. She was so aroused, she felt dizzy. He drew her up so she rose up on her knees. He crouched down before her and with his eyes on hers, he reached up under her skirt and drew her panties down to her knees. He leaned back slightly, his arm extending behind him. Her eyes widened at the scissors that with two metallic snips ruined her panties and left her bare in the office.

He tucked the scrap of fabric into the pocket of his jeans as he rose up, moving behind her. "Hands on the desk." She had to lean forward to do so and he drew her skirt up over her ass. One of his feet slid between her legs and pushed, opening her up.

"Doesn't get much more basic than this, does it? My pretty sub on her knees, ass bared to me and nerves dancing beneath her skin. The shit this week does not happen again, Katey Jay."

The light pull on her hair from being wrapped around his fist made it hard to concentrate. "I wasn't hiding from you. I was hiding from–"

"The shit this week," he said slowly, enunciating so she got the point, "does not happen again."

"No, Sir," she whispered.

"I don't care if we burn his house down or let it go, you sure as fuck don't sneak out of my bed and ignore texts. You do not beat yourself up for something beyond your control. You do not torture yourself." He bent over her, pulling her head back in an arch she felt pulling her entire body and he crushed his mouth to hers. "That is not how we work."

"I…I'm sorry."

"Good. Now, just in case you forget, I'm going to remind you that it's my job to beat on you and torture you."

Oh, Lord, she thought as he let her go. Fingers brushed over her ass. A gentle caress that made her heart sigh. Then came the hard snap against her ass. It was thin and painful. She cried out and her fingers gripped the edge of the desk as he rhythmically brought whatever torturous device he held down again and again. Her skin began to throb and burn and she lowered her head to her hands because this hurt. Yet beneath the spreading pain was a wicked wave of pleasure so intense it made her shake with need. The hard rock music that had been booming through the walls and door faded until it was just the sounds of her gasps and the punishing crack on her skin. Pain melted away. All the confusion and chaos of the past became insignificant compared to the absolute loneliness of being without him. Somehow, he had become important.

A tear slipped free, and another, and when a sob broke free she tried to muffle it. The spanking stopped and he bent over her, a protective wall between her and the world. "Let loose, Katey." Her fingers hurt when she slowly let go. He drew her up and onto his lap, sliding her skirt down over her ass. Her skin shuddered at the contact but it was insignificant as she wrapped an arm around his neck and buried her face against him.

Neither of them spoke as he held her, his hand gentle as it slid up and down her back. Finally the tears ran out and she sighed, resting her head on his shoulder. "I missed you," she whispered. It didn't matter that she had been sleeping at his house for the past week, she had put up walls. Between nightmares and her thoughts, she had, in a way, isolated herself even while being with him.

His thumb wiped over his cheek, a black drum stick still in his hand. No wonder it had hurt. "I wasn't the one who went away, Katey Jay."

"I know. I'm sorry. I don't know why I left. It was just overwhelming, I guess."

"What was? That I talked to someone or that I opened the box?"

She traced the three names forever imprinted on his heart. "That I wasn't alone with it. Only I *was* alone with it. My whole life it's just been me to rely on and then you came along and everything changed."

A fist hammered on the door, breaking apart the moment. "D, time to get to work."

"Damn it." He eased her off and adjusted the hem of her skirt. "You can watch from backstage or you can sit with Oz and Claire. Your call."

It would be so easy to say back stage. Usually she was anonymous in the crowd, invisible to all. "I'll sit with your friends." He grinned. Lowering his head, he kissed her. Not a sweet, hurried kiss, but a kiss full of hunger and promise.

"Oh the plans I have for you later." Setting his hand on her ass, he guided her out of the office, digging out his phone. "Texting Oz to fetch you because the odds of you finding him are slim."

"What kind of plans?"

He backed her against a wall, one arm braced above her as he loomed over her. His smile was wicked. "The kind that involves a cross, your naked ass and my crop."

Her breath was shaky as she exhaled slowly. Yet again

she found herself squeezing her thighs together and the slick skin from her arousal made her squirm. With the round head of his drum stick, he drew a line down her throat and between her breasts.

"Don't you sink into the ether when I'm about to go on stage and can't do a thing. Focus, Katey."

She blinked a few times until the soft, floaty feeling he caused ebbed away. "You're a bad man, Doyle Kolemann."

"It's what makes me a fantastic fucking dom." He tapped the stick against her stomach, a steady tempo as if the music was already moving through him.

"You're going to miss this. Aren't you?"

A big shoulder shrugged casually. "The music isn't going anywhere, sweetheart. I'm just ditching the baggage that comes with it."

An eyebrow arched up as she studied him, she believed that as much as she believed that elephants could fly. He bent his arm so he was closer. "Yes," he said in a soft, low voice, "I'm going to miss this."

"You don't have to quit the band, Doyle."

He nodded. "Yes, I do. More, I *need* to."

Rising up on her toes, she brushed her lips over his. "Go work." Before he could respond, she ducked under his arm and made her way to the stairs.

"Kate, do you have a moment?"

Surprised, she stared at Carl Hughes. She couldn't remember the last time she had talked to him and he certainly never sought her out. "Um." Fiddling with her bracelet, she glanced back over her shoulder and saw Doyle watching them, a drum stick lazily winding and spinning between and over his fingers. "I guess."

Considering someone had banged on the office door telling Doyle it was time to go on stage, no one appeared to be in any hurry to actually *be* on stage.

Carl folded his arms over his chest and narrowed his eyes. If he was going to blast her for breaking up the band like Jace had done, she very much feared she'd tell him to go fuck himself.

"Before you moved in with Jace, did he know about you?"

The question was so surprising, she didn't even hesitate in answering. "Yes." How could he not, considering the number of times her mom would hunt down his number, phone him and demand things like more money or taking her back. She never got either, which would send her into a rage and Kate would make herself scarce until her mom got lost in booze and drugs.

Carl didn't seem surprised by her answer. "So he knew you were around when we went to Beli's trailer? We went there, by the way. It was a sty."

Kate watched as she twisted a knot one way then the other, her fingers in constant nervous motion. A familiar hand slid under her hair to rest on the back of her neck. When Doyle caressed down her arm and covered her fingers, stopping her tell, she leaned back into him.

"He knew," she whispered, remembering hiding from them, so afraid of everything. Carl exhaled at her question, nodded and walked away, not that surprised. He knew because she had been the one to contact him that Belinda was dead and she was alone. She hadn't expected him to show up. She hadn't expected him to even look for her. Not that any of that hadn't kept her from wishing for something different. Wishing for someone different.

Wishing, period.

Strong arms wrapped around her. "You break my heart," Doyle said softly. He leaned against the wall, holding her. "That poor asshole."

Surprised at that statement, she tilted her head back and arched so she could see him.

"He missed out loving one helluva girl."

His words had the same effect on her as subspace. Everything felt calm within her, there was nothing but this moment. This moment with this man. Doyle. Dom. Reaching up she touched his cheek as she looked into his eyes. The round tip of his drumstick caressed along her throat. All her life she had looked for someone to give her love to her.

Her mother hadn't wanted it. Neither had Jace. Two terms battled within her: strike three you're out and third time's a charm. In her head she heard his voice from that night of the party, as if he was speaking now: *Breathe it in, hold, let it out.*

She took in his words, held them and finally let it out. "I love you."

He smiled, cupped his hand under her chin, and kissed her. "What did I tell you about me going on the stage and not being able to do a thing?" He rapped the drumstick against her nipple. His smile was downright wicked. "Good thing afterwards I'm going to beat on my pretty girl."

Epilogue

The Voice: And the beat goes on…with Katey Jay Designs
By Connor Evers

WHEN MY BROTHER asked if I wanted to interview Kate Jennings, I gave a solemn nod while I gave a mental fist pump. Why was I giving a mental fist pump over a woman named Kate Jennings? One who designs jewelry when this is a music column? Let's add a third name to that: Kate Jace Jennings.

Ringing any bells? Yes. As in Jace freakin' Jennings, lead singer of Cyanide. Anyone who reads my articles knows I am a huge Cyanide fan. High fives all around.

In 2001, news broke that Jennings had a daughter, before she disappeared from the limelight. Well, she's back, people, and if my brother says I should pay attention, I tend to listen. If I don't he'll wedgie me. Seriously.

First let me say this. I love my wife.

So when I found myself waiting at the doors to the flea market, I had to take a moment. One must always take a moment to appreciate when God makes something that fine. Yes…flea market. I was going shopping with the daughter of my rock god. The first thing I noticed, after getting over how much she looks like her famous father, was that she's quiet. This was an interview. I had to ask questions. That's my job.

Okay. Easy question. What was it like, I asked, to be the quintessential Cinderella? Rags to riches. From nobody to the daughter of Jace Jennings.

Mistake number one.

"I'm not nobody," she said, looking me dead in the eye. "I don't need to take shit from you."

My brother was going to kick. My. Ass. I mumbled an apology and she nodded at me and took me through the flea market. I was about to make mistake number two because my brother gave me nothing. Jensen Evers is an ass. Stop buying his art, Canada. He's a total dickwad.

I asked what it was like to be Jace Jennings' daughter.

She told me to go fuck myself only way more polite than that, then she walked off. I tweeted how my interview was going in the toilet. Instantly I got back:

Stop asking about her father, asshole. #doyourfuckingjob #youhurtheryoudie from @DoyleKole

Nothing says you're screwed like having your life threatened by a bad ass legend. So, shoving my phone away, I followed her. I love my wife. Remember this? I do. I've met some pretty sexy, beautiful ladies doing this job. None made me need to state to the world that I love my wife. But here's a fact I was about to learn: Kate Jennings is pretty damn easy to fall in love with.

I asked what I should've from the get go. Why were we prowling through a flea market? She smiled and that's it. I was done. Our first stop was a divey-looking little booth with a sketchy looking dude. Kate greeted him by name, introduced me, and pointed at a sad looking viola. How do I know it's a viola? She told me. It was missing a tuning peg and the front was scratched up by what could've been car keys. The sketchy dude told Kate he was saving it for her because he knew she would like it. It was a piece of trash. Why would she like it?

I'm so glad you asked, Canada. "Look at the grain," she said as she reverently ran her fingers down the neck. "It's that moment when the water's still before the ferry goes by. There had probably been a forest fire," she went on her voice less dreamy. "The trauma of it, the recovery, the regrowth. You know something's special when it can recover from trauma." She handed over five dollars and slid the viola into a cloth bag.

I knew I was in the presence of someone who had recovered, regrown. "How did you recover?"

She was quiet as we stopped at a second booth. She eyed a toy piano, waved and continued on. "Wounds heal. There's always the scar and the memory of it but the pain fades. That hurt...eventually fades." I asked what happened. She told me. The shitstorm on that trauma is hitting Vancouver now. I'll let you Google. I can't....what I saw in her eyes. I can't. The one holding her hand through this? Doyle Kole, Cyanide's drummer. Try that on for size, Canada, but at least I knew why he was threatening my life in tweets. [I trended.] But I was smarter then I was prior to our conversation. I didn't ask about Kole.

So the answer to why we were wandering around the flea market? Katey Jay Designs is all about music and jewelry. Half her life she grew up in the house of Canadian rock royalty and it took root. She's not a musician, she doesn't sing. But she takes the broken violas, the unwanted guitars, even used guitar picks, and makes some pretty cool jewelry. Recover. Regrowth.

I got to see her studio. It's awesome. Yeah, it pained my music lover's heart to see the innards of guitars on the walls, but the jewelry she makes is unique and cool. Want a piece of Cyanide history? There are a lot of their instruments in her jewelry. She's launching in the new year. Just in time for awards season. A fluke you ask? Nope, she said. "What comes with awards season? Swag bags." How did a not yet heard of jewelry designer from our beautiful city land in a swag bag? Two words according to her: "Jace. Jennings." Game, set, and match, Kate. Well played.

A week after I met her, a box showed up at The Voice. Inside? A bracelet for my wife made from the neck of that viola. What did I get? Cufflinks that were tuning pegs off one of Jace Jennings' guitars. High five to me. I'm off to wear a suit.

Like I said earlier: I love my wife.

But I'm a bit in love with Kate too.

[*Side note at time of printing: From @DoyleKole: @ ConnorEvers #yougettolive. This could change if he reads my column.*]

The Voice: And the beat goes on…with Doyle Kole
By Connor Evers

TO SAY THAT Doyle Kole is overwhelming is an understatement. The first time I met him I thought, "This dude is going to shank me in the night." He's big as hell, his ink is dark and twisted, and when he looks at you, you know he can put you in the ground. Impressive considering he's the former drummer of Cyanide instead of the MMA fighter he looks like, or you know, a prison escapee.

Say what you will about the rocker, he makes an impression when he sits down before you and you both wonder if the rinky dink wooden chair is going to hold him.

So here I am, in a trendy coffee shop in Vancouver of all places, with Cyanide's bad ass. Hello dream come true.

When news broke over a year and half ago that Kole was retiring from the band, I had a moment of utter denial. I may, or may not have, tweeted that he better be fucking joking to which I got a prompt reply of "I don't joke about fucking."

Funny guy.

Considering the animosity that had been apparent between him and the lead singer, Jace Jennings, in those last few years, I'm striking a reunion tour off my dream list. "We named the band after poison," Kole said as he leaned back in a chair that protested the movement. "That we went toxic shouldn't surprise anyone. You put five assholes in a room and we're going to slug it out. Tally that up for twenty-some-odd years and it was inevitable that we imploded." He has always been close-mouthed about that final implosion. Considering the death stares he can give, I opted against poking at that question. Much.

Ask him about retirement in his mid-forties and Kole will smirk without saying a word. Retirement is good for the musician. The man who looks like he'd mug you at the midnight hour is the father of three daughters. Three.

I can barely handle one boy. Two are teenagers from his first marriage. I shudder at the thought. Ask him about being a new dad in his forties. Go on. I dare you.

"I'm too old for this shit." He whipped out his phone to show me pictures of the fourteen-month old little girl who clearly has her daddy wrapped around her tiny little finger. I won't lie. I totally showed him pictures of my kid and we lost about thirty minutes as we high-fived each other about our awesome kids. Yes. I totally high-fived Doyle Kole. This hand. It's been gifted.

"I'm doing it differently. Not a redo because my girls are the best. Their mom did an amazing job with them since I was always gone. But this time I got my shit in line. I'm present now. With all of them. I'm a better man because of my girls."

Ask him about his pretty wife and things get a little dicier. He's protective and proud. She's the oldest daughter of Jace Jennings. In 2001, news broke that Jennings had a daughter with a former groupie who passed away from an overdose. After that we didn't see much of Kate (née Jennings) Kole until late-2015 when she began rocking out some amazingly cool jewelry as Katey Jay Designs. The store, I might add, is right across the street from where we sat, and if you remember correctly you heard about her here first. Spoiler alert: I lived.

A tip for everyone: Do not, I repeat, do not call her Katey or you will learn about the fear sweats. "Kate," was all he said, staring at me and daring me to argue with him. Please, Mrs. Kate [I'll never refer to you as Katey again but remember how much I love you?] Kole, don't let your husband kill me. My wife thinks I'm awesome. They're expecting baby number two in a few months. I can't even…safe sex, kids. Safe sex.

Deciding that not pissing Kole off about his wife's name was a good thing, I took it back to music.

With former Cyanide guitarist Maximillian Jones, Kole joined ranks with some pretty rocking names down in Seattle. The commute is short and the band, Ravage, plays locally and along the Pacific Northwest. The time for lengthy world tours, Kole said, was for the young. They're leaving the road open to the next generation. "Max and Carl's [Carl Hughes was Cyanide's lead guitarist] boys are taking over. Hysteria, check them out." Hysteria, if anyone remembers, and you had better, opened for Cyanide at Kole's final and may I add epic show at Wallace's, a local music hot spot here in Vancouver. A passing of the torch to the next generation. It's one helluva torch too. Twenty-six years of some pretty awesome rock. Eighteen albums. A couple of Grammys, four Junos, a star on Canada's Walk of Fame and an induction into Canada's Music Hall of Fame later this year. Start practicing boys, you've got some mighty big shoes to fill. Especially Kole's. I think he wears size twenty. Seriously. How much milk did he drink as a kid?

[Side note at time of printing: Why yes, we did spend fifteen more minutes looking at pictures of our kids. He told me that I better hope my son didn't date his daughter when they were older. Mikey, sorry but if you love your old man, no Koles for you. We high-fived our awesome DNA again. I went home and listened to Horned *with the wife. Baby number two is on its way. Damn it. Safe sex, kids. Safe sex.]*

**Want more for your naughty to be read pile?**

Scorpio Stings
Scoring Lacey
Sarah Mine

And on the deliciously naughty BDSM side
Domme for Cowboy

The Edge Series
Claimed Book 1
Tempt Book 2: a novella
Yield Book 3

Erotica
Her Surrender

Bio

Jenna's writing dreams truly began one summer on the air mattress of her childhood home. There she tackled her first romance: a truly wretched attempt at a medieval historical. Upon finishing the purple prose laden story of (in her own words) crap, Jenna decided that perhaps the historical genre wasn't for her and she promptly began to write in a contemporary setting. If only the journey had been easy. She tackled category romances (and in her own words) felt like they were crap. She didn't have the patience for romantic suspense. Really, she just wanted to get to writing the sex. (hint hint, Jenna) Her romantic comedies were so traumatic that she stopped writing until one day she got a phone call from a friend who said "We can totally write this." The genre was erotic romance and it was (in her own words) like coming home. Residing in Calgary, Alberta, Jenna happily writes the naughty romances that make her mother sooooo comfortable. (not)

www.jennahoward.com